## LOOK OUT FOR THE WHOLE SERIES!

Case Files 11 & 12: The Case of the Medieval Meathead & The Case of the Messy Mucked Up Masterpiece

Case Files 13 & 14: The Case of the Guy Who Makes You Act Like a Chicken & The Case of the Felon with Frosty Fingers

Case Files 15 & 16: The Case of the Bogus Banknotes & The Case of Eight Arms and No Fingerprints

Case Files 17 & 18: The Case of the Flowers That Make Your Body All Wobbly & The Case of the Guy Who Looks Pretty Good for a 2000 Year-Old

Case Files 19 & 20: The Case of the Gobbling Goop & The Case of the Surfer Dude Who's Truly Rude

Case Files 21 & 22: The Case of the Cactus, the Coot, and the Cowboy Boot & The Case of the Seal Who Gets All Up In Your Face

Case Files 23 & 24: The Case of the Snow, the Glow, and the Oh, No! & The Case of the Fish That Flew the Coop

# THE CASE OF THE
# FUDGIE FRY PIRATES

Hodder
Children's
Books

A division of Hachette Children's Books

## Special thanks to Lucy Courtenay
## and Artful Doodlers

Copyright © 2008 Chorion Rights Limited, a Chorion company

First published in Great Britain in 2008 by Hodder Children's Books

2

A Catalogue record for this book is available from the British Library

ISBN 978 0 340 95977 0

Typeset in Weiss by Avon DataSet Ltd,
Bidford on Avon, Warwickshire

Printed in Great Britain by
Clays Ltd, St Ives plc

The paper and board used in this paperback by Hodder Children's
Books are natural recyclable products made from wood grown in
sustainable forests. The manufacturing processes conform to the
environmental regulations of the country of origin.

Hodder Children's Books
a division of Hachette Children's Books
338 Euston Road, London NW1 3BH
An Hachette Livre UK Company
www.hachettelivre.co.uk

# Chapter One

A seven-metre sailboat sat on wooden supports outside the shed. Wearing grungy clothes, a toolbelt and a cap, Jo was in a suspended bosun's chair halfway up the boat's mast, polishing it with a cloth. Her elbow was starting to hurt.

"You've started, so you've got to finish," Jo told herself firmly, pushing her brown hair behind her ears.

She glanced down to where a large and very hairy dog was snoozing in the shade cast by the boat's hull. "You've got it right, Timmy," she sighed, wiping her forehead.

Timmy woofed gently and rolled on to his back.

"Be careful up there, Jo," warned Jo's mum George, who was potting something bushy in a terracotta tub down in the yard below. "If you fall, you'll crush my Devil's Moustache."

"Thanks for the concern, Mum," Jo said sarcastically. She turned back to the mast and rubbed it hard. "Shine!" she growled. "Shine more!"

She slapped the mast with her cloth in frustration. "Whoa!"

Jo's sudden movement made her chair wobble. She dropped her polishing cloth and flailed her arms as she and the chair went spinning head over heels, getting tangled in the boat's ropes.

Timmy leaped to his feet and started barking fiercely. Jo grabbed the mast and used it to spin herself back in the other direction. She did a neat backflip out of her bonds and landed on the ground like a gymnast, missing the Devil's Moustache by a whisker.

"I'll get this shipshape before Max and Allie and Dylan get here if it kills me," Jo said. She slapped the boat, which promptly toppled over on top of her. "Which it just might do," she added in a muffled voice.

2

The honk of a taxi horn floated down from a nearby hilltop.

"Oh!" said Jo in excitement. "They're coming!"

She struggled to push the boat off her as the taxi trundled into view, pursued by a tall blond boy on a mountain bike pedalling for all he was worth.

"Attaboy, Timmy," Jo said, scrambling free as Timmy tugged her arm. "Oh, I hope everyone's ready to have some cool adventures! I've got a lot of things planned."

Her jumper caught on the boat and unravelled. George raised her eyebrows.

"What?" said Jo. "I can have adventures with half a jumper."

"Whoo!" shouted Max, pedalling like fury behind the taxi. There was no way he was going to let Allie and Dylan get to Jo's house first.

Swerving off the road, Max plunged down the side of a hill, jumped a fence and started slaloming through some startled cows. "'Scuse me!" he shouted. "Pardon me, ladies! Short cut!"

The hill suddenly got steeper. Max twisted his wheels and took off, straight through the middle of a hay cart. Coughing and trailing haystalks, he landed on the other side and continued on his downward plunge.

The taxi containing his cousins was almost at Jo's gate. Putting on a fresh burst of speed, Max twisted his handlebars one more time and leaped over another fence, landing in Jo's yard just as the taxi pulled up.

"Hey, Jo!" Max called, squealing his bike to a halt. "It's so great to be here!"

His front tyre hit an upturned rake lying in the

middle of the yard. The tyre exploded and the bike stopped abruptly, causing Max to fly over the handlebars towards the boat and hit his head on the ship's bell.

*Dong!!*

"That's going to sting a while," said Max, rubbing his head woozily. "Hey, great boat, though! Really brilliant!"

Dylan kicked open the taxi door. He was holding a DVD camera in one hand, his dark hair flopping to one side.

"Max, bash into that boat again," he said. "I can sell the footage to 'World's Wackiest Wipe-Outs'. Do you think you could bleed a bit?" he added seriously. "That'd really help me out."

Allie scrambled out of the taxi. "Hey Jo!" she said happily, her blond hair bouncing on her shoulders and her pretty skirt somehow totally uncreased. "Love your half-a-sweater! What a neat style! Hi, Aunt George!"

"Lovely to see you, dears!" George smiled, waving her potted plant. "I'll go and get lunch ready."

Allie eyed the plant. "Is that some kind of . . . salad, Aunt George?"

"I won't be feeding you my Devil's Moustache," George laughed. "It's toxic – it would make your hair fall out and your teeth turn black. Of course," she added vaguely as she breezed into the house, "my pork pies aren't much better."

"I didn't think you'd ever get here!" Jo said breathlessly to her cousins. "How was your trip?"

"Fun!" Allie laughed. "I think Dylan taped the whole train ride, if you actually want to see it."

Dylan lowered his camera. "I'm looking for reality show ideas," he said, adjusting his glasses. "'Americans on British Trains' didn't work out, but reality's all around. Let's see . . ."

He panned around the yard. Timmy was leaping about, trying to catch a butterfly with his mouth.

"I've got it!" said Dylan in triumph, zooming in. "'World's Most Dangerous Dogs'!"

Timmy looked embarrassed and pretended he had been yawning.

"Or . . ." said Dylan, swinging around a little further as a frail, middle-aged postman puffed towards them on his bike, a package in the handlebar basket. "'Exhausted Delivery Men and Their Secrets'?"

"Aaah," panted the postman, wheezing as he leaned his bike against the gate. "Allie Campbell? I've been trying to flag you down since you left the train station – I waved and waved and . . ."

"I thought you were being friendly," Allie said. "That's why I waved back."

"Indeed," sniffed the postman. "Sign here, please."

Allie scribbled her name and took her package. "It's from my friend Courtney, back home!" she told the others. "We always send each other presents." She opened the box and stared at the brown contents. "No way!" she gasped. "It's from our favourite candy store!" She frowned and peered closer. "Fudgie Fries?" she said. "Nobody likes Fudgie Fries."

"That's because they taste like brown ear-wax fried in pig slobber," said Jo.

BOOM!

Everyone jumped.

"What was that?" said Dylan in excitement, grabbing his camera again. "Did a meteorite slam into the earth? That'd be cool footage!"

Jo shimmied up a ladder to the shed roof. Now she could see over the tree line, down towards the

7

beach and beyond, to a mysterious green island hunkered offshore.

"Whoa!" Jo gasped. "That came from Shelter Island. But it's supposed to be deserted!"

The others scrambled up the ladder to join her. Panting slightly, Timmy followed.

"Brilliant!" Max said enthusiastically. "Let's go there tomorrow!"

"And I'll bring dessert," Allie offered, waving the box of Fudgie Fries.

"Why wait till tomorrow?" Jo said eagerly. "Why not go right now?"

CRUNNNCCHH! The roof caved in beneath them.

"Whoah!" shouted the cousins, falling straight through and landing on a pile of straw below.

" 'Cos I think we need to fix the roof first," Dylan coughed.

# Chapter Two

Jo and her cousins hurried down to the shore as soon as they'd finished breakfast the next day. Stretching out into the water was a wooden dock, where several fishing smacks and little dinghies were moored. Jo's boat was among them.

Jo stroked her boat's gleaming wooden hull. She felt proud that she had polished it from top to toe.

"Ready?" she asked the others.

Everyone nodded. Dylan lifted his camera as Jo handed Allie a bottle of ginger beer.

Allie cleared her throat. "I hereby christen thee . . ." she began, lifting the bottle and preparing to smash it against the side of the boat. She stopped. "Oh," she said. "We need a name for the boat, don't we?"

"How about 'Weird Exploding Mystery Island Boat'?" said Max eagerly. "Or 'WEMIB' for short!"

Timmy whined and tucked his nose under his paws.

"Hmm," said Jo, folding her arms and looking unimpressed. "How about, 'no'?"

"Got it!" Allie exclaimed. "I hereby christen thee, 'Jo's Boat'!"

She started to swing the bottle at the prow.

"Stop!" said Dylan suddenly. "Don't do that!"

"Why not?" said Max in surprise.

"That's ginger beer," said Dylan, snatching the bottle. "And I'm thirsty. Anybody have a bottle opener?"

"Ye can use me hook!" boomed a gruff voice behind them.

Jo and the others whirled round to see a wild-eyed man with long black hair and a beard standing on the dockside. His head was covered with a bandana, his trousers were tucked into seaboots, and his shirt billowed in the wind as he waved his hook menacingly at them.

"Eeep!" Allie squeaked.

The pirate snatched the bottle from Dylan. "Ah," he said after a minute. " 'Tis a twist-off."

He opened the bottle and handed it back to Dylan. Then he twisted off his hook, revealing a large pink hand. "Pirate Dan, and fairly met," he said with a gold-toothed grin, holding out his hand to shake.

"Daniel and I are in the same yoga class," said George, coming along the dockside. "He runs a souvenir shop on the harbour."

"Here," said Pirate Dan, fumbling in his coat pocket. "Have a free eye patch."

He handed the eye patches round. Allie giggled and put hers on Timmy's right eye. Timmy woofed in confusion and trotted straight into the dustbin in the middle of the dock.

CLONG!

Looking dizzy, Timmy backed away and sat down to steady himself – too near the edge of the dock. His legs pedalled thin air as he slipped over the edge and down into a boatload of flopping fish.

As everyone roared with laughter at Timmy,

Pirate Dan handed Jo a skull-and-crossbones flag, which billowed in the wind. "As yer the cap'n, I brought this fer ya," he said. "I fly one just like it on my boat."

"What are we waiting for?" Max said, rubbing his hands as Timmy clambered back on to the dock, looking embarrassed. "We have a flag, we have a boat, we have an explosion that I'll bet was a crashed UFO with lizardy aliens . . ."

Timmy shook himself. Fish flew out from under his shaggy coat. Amazingly, Allie caught one.

". . . and we have haddock for lunch!" Allie finished with a grin.

The flag flew from the masthead as Jo, Max, Allie, Dylan and Timmy sailed towards Shelter Island. The weather was brisk, with a fresh wind buffeting the sails. Jo was at the helm, and Dylan was avidly filming the view.

"The wind's changing," Jo said. "OK guys. Reef the jenny, move the traveller on the boomvang and trim the mainsail."

"Great!" Max beamed. "But I have no idea what you just said."

Timmy woofed as the others looked at Jo blankly as well.

Jo tutted. "Crank the round thingy, push the curly dingus over, and oh – pull that rope-y doo-dah. Got it?"

Timmy barked encouragement as Allie cranked a winch which moved the boom.

"Oh!" Allie puffed, letting go of the winch to wipe her brow. "My arms are out of breath!"

The boom immediately unwound and whipped across the boat. Timmy flung himself down on the deck as the boom swooped past and smacked Max in the head as he coiled a line to a cleat.

"Oops," Allie wailed.

"Man!" Max yelled, releasing his line and clutching his head. "That's going to sting a while."

The rope uncoiled from the cleat like a snake and wrapped around Max's foot, hoisting him up the mast as the jib sail collapsed in a heap on Dylan's head.

"OK," said Dylan in a muffled voice. "That's a cut."

"Ahoy!" came a gasping voice. The sound of oars slapping the water floated over to the boat. "Ahoy! A-whew!"

Badly winded, the old postman rowed alongside Jo and the others in a small boat. "Delivery for Allie Campbell," he wheezed, paddling closer and waving his clipboard. "Again," he added, sounding not too pleased about it. "Sign, please."

Allie reached over to sign the clipboard. The postman shipped the oars and stretched up to meet her. His little boat began to drift away, causing him to stretch a bit too far.

"Oh dear . . ." said the postman, waving his arms to regain his balance. "Ahhh . . ."

SPLASH!

The four cousins and Timmy rushed to the side of the boat.

"Are you OK?" Jo called anxiously.

The postman surfaced and thrashed his arms in the sea. "Hit it, Danny," he spluttered to a boy clutching a guitar in the back of his delivery boat.

"Oh golly," Allie gasped, as the boy broke into song. "It's Danny Scott!"

"My best friend Allie is away," the boy sang. His hair hung over his eyes and he strummed his guitar enthusiastically. "Here's what happened at camp today . . ."

14

"Oh golly," moaned Allie in ecstasy.

"Our counsellor's name is Mrs Goff," sang Danny Scott, still strumming hard as the postman struggled back into the boat. "She sneezed so hard her wig came off, in Whitney Alcott's SOUUP!" He gave a final flourish on his guitar. "Thank you," he called, bowing to Allie and raising his hands. "Thank you, England!"

WHACK!

"Aah," yelled the postman, falling back into the sea as Danny Scott's guitar swung back and knocked him off the boat again.

"Well," said Jo with a shrug, "if you ask me, power tools make a better gift."


On a rocky bluff on the coast of Shelter Island, a tall blond man watched the boat approach. He pulled a walkie-talkie out of his pocket.

"HQ, this is Kyle," he snarled into the walkie-talkie. "There's some kids sailing towards Green Cove. Must've heard the explosion. I think we should arrange a little welcome party. Har, har, har . . ."

He stopped laughing and studied his walkie-

15

talkie for a moment. "Hang on," he muttered. "Is this on?"

He pressed a few buttons. The walkie-talkie sparked and fizzed, making his hair stand on end.

"G'ah!" Kyle shouted, clutching his hand and dropping the walkie-talkie in the sand.

# Chapter Three

The kids and Timmy moored their boat offshore and rowed to Shelter Island's beach in their dinghy. They hiked along a bluff toward an old, decrepit lighthouse that poked like a broken needle into the sky. Timmy glanced around, growling uneasily.

"I haven't seen anything that could have caused that 'boom' noise," said Dylan, shouldering his camera.

"Did you know the government has secret invisibility machines?" said Max in an excited voice. "Maybe one blew up!"

Jo frowned over her shoulder at Max. "Just how hard did you hit your head on that boat?" she checked.

The path rose steeply. Puffing and scrambling over the rocks, they reached the abandoned lighthouse. Jo pushed open the door, which creaked and groaned like a creature in pain. A rickety wooden staircase wound along the inner wall, leading to the top.

"Let's go up," said Allie. "Maybe from there we can see the invisible machine that exploded!"

She started climbing the old wooden stairs. The others followed. Timmy, however, stayed below. As he watched them go, he heard a strange, high-pitched drone. Whining, he shook his head. The drone didn't go away. He tried barking instead, but that didn't work either.

The kids climbed on up the steps. It looked as if they hadn't noticed the drone at all.

"Our counsellor's name is Mrs Goff," Jo sang quietly to herself. "She sneezed so hard her wig fell off . . ." She stopped. "That stupid song's stuck in my head!" she complained.

"Drink a glass of water," Max murmured woozily. "That cures it. Or maybe that's hiccups . . ."

Timmy was shaking his head, irritated by the droning noise. "WOOF!" he barked up at the kids, scrabbling at the steps. "WOOF!"

Ignoring Timmy, the cousins reached the top of the stairs, arriving at a railed platform at the top of the lighthouse. There was a thirty-five metre drop down to crashing waves at the base of a rocky cliff below.

"Oooh," Jo mumbled. "I feel a little strange. What about you guys?"

"Take the plunge . . ." Allie murmured, staring glassily over the edge of the railing.

"Jump," Dylan whispered.

"Jump," Max repeated dreamily.

Dylan's fingers went limp and he dropped his camera. It went bouncing down the stairs, past Timmy – and was caught by a big man with bushy hair and a furious expression on his face, who had just stepped into the lighthouse.

"Hey!" Kyle yelled, waving his arms and looking red-faced with rage. "Get down from there! It's dangerous!"

Timmy barked as Kyle grabbed a hose and turned on the tap. Pointing the hose up the stairs at the kids, he blasted them all with a jet of water.

"Ugh!" Max shouted, shaking his head.

"I don't feel strange now," said Jo, staring down at her soggy clothes. "Now I feel wet." She yelled down the stairs: "Hey! Enough water! We get it! We're leaving!"

"You kids shouldn't be here," ranted Kyle, rubbing his massive hands through his hair as he led the kids to the path down the bluffs. Allie trailed behind her cousins, rapidly stuffing her face with Fudgie Fries. "This island's off-limits!"

"Why?" Jo demanded.

Kyle's eyes nearly popped out of his head. "Why?!" he shouted. "IT'S A BLOOMIN' PUFFIN REFUGE, THAT'S WHY! DID I SPEND MY LIFE STUDYING PUFFINS SO A BUNCH OF KIDS COULD COME STOMPING AROUND SCARING THEM? I DID NOT!"

The path shook beneath the cousins' feet as Kyle shouted at them.

"Maybe that 'boom' yesterday was him," Allie murmured to Jo between mouthfuls of Fudgie Fries.

Max nudged Dylan's arm and motioned with his head. Dylan stared at the dagger tattoo on Kyle's forearm.

"We just came to find out what that explosion was the other day," Dylan said, tearing his eyes away from the tattoo.

"A generator blew out," said Kyle shortly.

"Must've been a big generator," Jo said.

Kyle's eyes boggled again. "'COURSE IT'S A BIG GENERATOR!" he roared. "YOU'VE GOT TO HAVE POWER FOR THE INCUBATORS, OR THE PUFFINS WON'T HATCH! THEN THERE'S NO MORE PUFFINS! DO I WANT

A WORLD WITH NO MORE PUFFINS? I DO NOT!"

He stomped off ahead of them.

"There's something fishy about that guy," said Jo.

"Forget him," said Max, waving his hand. "We'll say goodbye to Mr Screaming Bird-kook, and sail somewhere else tomorrow."

A fierce storm raged the following day. Lightning zigzagged through the sky, and the thunder cracked and rippled the air.

Back at Jo's house, Jo, Dylan and Allie sat in George's study and watched the pouring rain through the windows. Allie was still making her way through her Fudgie Fries. Lying on the rug, Max and Timmy were playing draughts.

"Well, we won't be sailing anywhere today, thank you very much, rain," Jo sighed.

Max moved a piece. Timmy promptly pushed one of his pieces and quadruple-jumped Max, clearing the board.

"Ah, you win again, Timmy dude," said Max, scratching his head. "How 'bout five out of eight?"

"Anybody want a Fudgie Fry?" Allie mumbled

between mouthfuls. "For some reason I just can't stop eating 'em."

Timmy sniffed a Fudgie Fry which had fallen on the floor. He whined in disgust and drop-kicked it into the wastebasket in the corner.

"Allie, those aren't even real fudge," Max said. "They're like, ground-up goat hooves and artificial chemicals, then they deep-fry them in fat." He scrambled to his feet and flung himself at the box. "Mmmm," he mumbled. "I want one!"

"When I'm your age, will I crave rubbish foods?" Dylan said to Max in confusion.

"How do you like my Giant Biaclarata?" asked George, coming into the study with a large potted plant in her hands. "If its thorns stick you, the poison will make you go all rubbery and you can't stop burping." She held it up proudly. "Who wants to feed it mice?"

Allie looked green and pushed the Fudgie Fries away. "We'd love to, Aunt George," she mumbled, "but, um . . . we gotta go!"

The cousins scurried out of the study, whizzing past George in every direction.

"Whoa!" said George, losing her grip on the

Giant Biaclarata and pricking her nose on a poisonous thorn. "Oh, dear," she said faintly, her body going rubbery. "Timmy, be a love (BURP!) and fetch my (BURP!) antidote case. I've gone a bit (BURP!) rubbery (BURP!) . . ."

# Chapter Four

The storm clouds raced above the ocean. Allie and Dylan were wrestling to steer Jo's boat through the towering waves. Hanging on tightly, Dylan wielded his camera at Allie, who gave a forced grin and addressed the lens.

"Hi, it's Allie, your Puffin Girl!" she said. "We're headed for Shelter Island!" She paused and looked at Dylan. "Are you sure this is a good idea?" she said. " 'Cos I'd rather have gone to the movies with Jo and Max."

"The Nature Channel will pay a fortune for puffin footage," said Dylan firmly, struggling to hold the camera as the waves lashed across the deck. "You heard the angry guy – 'THEY'RE BLOOMIN' ENDANGERED'!"

A flash of lightning lit up the stormy sky.

"Right now," Allie moaned, "so are we!"

From the tree-line on Shelter Island, Kyle was watching the boat with rage all over his face. He tore his walkie-talkie from his belt.

"Those rotten kids are coming back," he said. "This time we won't go so easy on 'em." Tutting, he shook the gadget and held it to his ear. "Don't tell me it's not on *again*?"

*Weeeeeaaaahscreeee!* wailed the feedback on the walkie-talkie.

"Aaghh!" howled Kyle, hurling the walkie-talkie away in disgust. It bounced off a rock, rebounded and hit him in the head, knocking him over just as Allie and Dylan sailed up to the shoreline – and straight into danger!

Max tucked his skateboard under his arm as he and Jo approached the Falcongate Cinema manager, Mr Grubbins.

"Hey," said Jo, whacking her hands down on the

26

ticket desk.

"Huh!" Mr Grubbins, the sweaty, jittery cinema manager leaped out of his skin, scattering the box of jelly beans he was eating.

"The film was supposed to start forty-five minutes ago!" said Jo.

Grubbins looked even sweatier. "Um . . ." he said, scratching his large tummy. "A fuse blew in the projector."

"Fifteen minutes ago you said the bulb had burned out," Jo said, frowning.

"What are you accusing me of?" said Mr Grubbins, sounding panicky. "If you don't like the service, you can have your money back." He pushed the cash across the counter. "Now go away. You're activating my twitch."

Sure enough, Mr Grubbins' face started twitching as he shooed Jo and Max towards the door. He rushed back to his ticket booth and reached for the phone.

"Mr Twitchy's awfully nervous," said Jo, pausing at the door.

Max pulled a face. "And his money sure is sweaty . . ." He held out the money, which dripped on the cinema carpet.

A figure in a raincoat pushed through the door with a stack of film cans, barging past Jo and Max. The hood of the raincoat was obscuring his face, but Max noticed the dagger tattoo on the figure's forearm. He grabbed Jo and pulled her behind some cardboard cutouts of a female Space Ranger with a laser gun and a big, purple alien with three eyes and five arms.

The figure approached Mr Grubbins.

"Finally," said Mr Grubbins, his eyes darting around the lobby. "Have you got my film?"

"It's the guy from the island!" Max whispered, just as Kyle pushed back his hood.

"DON'T TELL ME I'M LATE!" Kyle shouted, red-faced and waving his arms. "I CAN'T CONTROL THE WEATHER, CAN I? AM I A WEATHER GOD? NO I AM NOT!"

"Or he has an angry twin," Jo said.

"I'm taking a big risk letting you use my films," Mr Grubbins was saying to Kyle. "Makes me twitch."

Jo and Max glanced at each other. They moved the cutouts so they could hear better, making it look like the Space Ranger and the alien were walking across the lobby.

"WHAT ABOUT MY RISKS?" Kyle bellowed. "WOULD I WANT THE POLICE TO FIND THE MERCHANISE IN MY CAR? I WOULD NOT!"

Max and Jo stared wide-eyed at each other. What was this about?

Suddenly Max's phone went off. *Rinnnggg! Rinnnggg!* Max turned it off as fast as he could. But it was too late.

"What was that?" Mr Grubbins said.

# Chapter Five

The Space Ranger and the alien appeared to panic as Jo and Max bumped into each other, fell down, scrambled back up and shuffled across the lobby to the snack bar.

Kyle and Mr Grubbins started toward the cutouts just as Max and Jo ducked behind the snack bar counter. Max pulled the nozzle off a slushy machine. Jo opened the popcorn machine. Still hiding behind the bar, they hit the switches.

Blue slush and hot popcorn began to whoosh over the counter, hitting Kyle and Mr Grubbins.

"THIS POPCORN HURTS!" Kyle shrieked, covering his head with his arms as the popcorn bounced down. "IS THIS REAL BUTTER? IT IS NOT! IT'S FAKE BUTTER FLAVOURING! *FAKE!* NOW I'M *REALLY* MAD!"

As Kyle and Mr Grubbins flailed around in the slippery blue popcorny mush, Max and Jo slipped through the back exit of the cinema.

It had stopped raining. Max and Jo spotted a car parked in the alley outside. There was a cartoon puffin painted on the side panel. A big guy sat behind the wheel, eating a sandwich.

"Kyle's car!" Jo guessed. "I want to see that 'merchandise'. Distract the driver," she ordered Max.

Max nodded. He jumped on to his skateboard and rolled towards the car. Turning, Max grinned at Jo and flashed her a thumbs-up. Then he leaped off his board, over the front end of the car . . . and crashed into a stack of egg crates and vegetable boxes behind a restaurant on the other side.

As Max woozily wiped egg yolk and tomatoes from his face, he glanced at the driver to see how his ploy had worked. The driver was busy wiping mustard off his shirt. He had completely missed Max's stunt.

Max raised his arms helplessly at Jo.

31

"Again!" Jo mouthed, gesturing at the car.

Max clambered to his feet and skated towards a cargo ramp at the far end of the alley. He launched into the air, did a graceful flip – and this time, got tangled in a line of laundry that was stretched across the alley. Max struggled to free himself from an old lady's dress that had somehow wrapped itself around him as the driver reset his radio dial. He had missed Max again!

Sighing, Max clambered down and tried one last

time. He flung himself at the car's windscreen, pressing his face into the glass.

"Mmwap's ffoim moo hing muhwhyme!" he mumbled.

The driver leaped out of the car. "Cripes!" he said. "You okay, kid?"

"Ow," Max moaned in his most convincing voice. "I broke all my bones! I broke my stomach, I broke my kidneys!"

Jo sneaked to the back of the car and opened the boot. It was stacked with DVDs called *Just Plane Crazy Fool*, which had a cartoon pelican flying a plane on the front cover. Nestling next to the DVDs was a large case of Fudgie Fries.

"DVDs?" said Jo, confused.

Max pulled his phone out of his pocket. "I should call the hospital," he slurred at the driver. "My vision's blurry, I can't hear, my taste buds are broken!"

Jo peeped around the edge of the car and gave Max the thumbs-up. Max snapped his phone sharply shut.

"I'm better now," he grinned at the driver, before scampering away. "Cheerio!"

"Stupid kid," the driver muttered. "Got nose sweat on me windscreen."

Max tore around the corner to find Jo.

"DVDs of *Just Plane Crazy Fool*," Jo explained. "That film isn't out yet. Whatever Old Angry Nut-Bag is doing on that island, it's not protecting puffins. And I bet it's illegal!"

Max noticed a blinking light on his phone. "Hey," he said, "I've got a voicemail . . ."

He checked the message on speaker.

"Hi, it's Allie," chirped Allie's voice. "Funny story – Dylan and I are sailing to Shelter Island, and the boat keeps making a 'nngraaaack' sound? Is that bad? Also is there a toilet on board?"

Jo grabbed Max's phone and dialled.

"It says 'mobile unit is not responding'," she said after a minute. "Those guys on the island are dangerous – Allie and Dylan have no idea what they're sailing towards!"

# Chapter Six

Dylan, Allie and Timmy trudged towards the lighthouse on Shelter Island. Allie was wearing a rucksack and carrying a bag of Fudgie Fries.

"Quit eating all the Fudgie Fries," said Dylan, taking the bag from her.

Allie flapped her hands at him. "Take 'em. They're so grossly bad for me." She paused and reached out again. "On second thoughts, give 'em back!"

"We've been halfway around this island, and we haven't seen one single puffin," Dylan sighed, giving the Fudgie Fries back to Allie. He paused. "What does a puffin look like?" he asked.

"They're kind of penguin-y," Allie mumbled, her mouth full. "With more of a parrot nose going on. Maybe the exploding generator scared them away."

A strange noise floated across the air towards them. It was the sound of roaring aircraft and laser cannons blasting. Timmy whined and put his head on one side, looking puzzled.

"Or the galactic space battle might have done it," Dylan suggested.

They entered the lighthouse cautiously. Now they could clearly hear the unmistakable sound of rocket ships and ray guns.

"All right, star scum," rasped a voice out of sight. "Hands up!"

Dylan and Allie stared around. There was nothing there!

Timmy growled at the floor. He pawed it, and poked at various points where the flagstones met each other. Then he barked as a spring-loaded trapdoor flew open, squashing Timmy underneath it as it slammed to the floor.

"It's coming from the trapdoor!" said Allie, rushing over to the dark space that was revealed at their feet. "Good job, Timmy!"

"Woof," Timmy growled weakly, struggling out from beneath the door.

"I knew it was there," Dylan said confidently. "I let Timmy find it 'cos I like to encourage his curiosity."

Both Allie and Timmy rolled their eyes as Dylan hunkered down and peered into the dark space.

A large, underground cave with a wooden staircase leading down from where they were standing had been revealed. The cave was full of tele-cine machines for transferring film to DVD. These were the source of the strange sounds. Another area was devoted to computers, which burned films on to DVD. A handful of technicians were monitoring the operation.

"I knew something was up!" Dylan whispered, filming with his camera as he, Allie and Timmy cautiously made their way down the stairs. "They're burning bootleg DVDs. These guys are pirating films!"

"Oooh," said Allie in excitement. "I hope they have *Hip Hoppin' High*!"

Dylan lowered his camera and stared at his cousin.

"C'mon," said Allie. "Who doesn't love *Hip Hoppin' High*?"

Below them in the cave, a technician was approaching a colleague.

"We're burning another thousand copies of *Just Plane Crazy Fool*," he said, his voice carrying up to where Allie, Dylan and Timmy were standing. "I need the hypno-frequency disc."

The other technician handed over a CD. "Here," he said with a smirk. "Talk about your 'hidden extras' on a DVD . . ."

"Hypno-frequency?" Dylan said. "That's an ultrasonic tone they use to brainwash people!"

"*Just Plane Crazy Fool*'s a kids' film," said Allie. "If they're embedding that hypno-thingy in kids' DVDs, that means they're brainwashing kids!"

Dylan's eyes blazed with excitement. "What a great idea for a reality show!" he gasped. "*Brainwashers and Bamboozlers*. I'm going to make a fortune!"

Allie folded her arms and looked at Dylan with her eyebrows raised.

"Though we all know brainwashing is wrong," Dylan said hastily. "Very, very wrong."

"All right, you two," came an angry-sounding

voice. "Don't even think about escaping."

Dylan peered around through his camera. "What film is that from?" he said, still gazing down at the machines.

Allie tugged Dylan's sleeve and pointed behind him. Looking displeased, Kyle was standing above them on the stairs.

"Oh," said Dylan, lowering his camera as Kyle reached down to grab them. "It's from *Dylan and Allie are Completely Stuffed . . .*"

# Chapter Seven

Back on the mainland, Max and Jo were trying on pirate outfits in Pirate Dan's souvenir shop. The whole place was filled with pirate souvenirs: flags, rubber swords, skulls and treasure chests.

"Of course we can take my boat to find your cousins!" Pirate Dan roared, scratching his nose with the end of his hook. He was still dressed in full pirate costume. "The pirate code requires me to lend assistance to a friend in distress."

Jo frowned. "Ah no," she corrected, "the pirate code was robbing people, sinking their ships and pillaging their towns."

There was a pause. Max hopped past on a pair of

Pirate Dan's pretend peg legs and crashed into a display bin of spiky pufferfish.

"That was the old code," Pirate Dan said at last, as Max sheepishly scrambled to his feet. "We changed it for the tourist trade. Me boat's moored yonder."

He stumped over to the window and flung open the shutters. Max and Jo gasped in amazement. Moored outside was a full-scale replica of *Queen Anne's Revenge*, Blackbeard's pirate ship.

"Whoa," said Max, brushing pufferfish off his shoulders, "that's your boat?"

Pirate Dan beamed. "Ya like it?" he said proudly. "I built it from a kit."

Back on Shelter Island, Dylan pushed his way through the boxes of CDs, old electronic gear, office stationery and supplies that filled the underground chamber where he, Timmy and Allie had been imprisoned. He tested the handle on the locked door. It didn't budge.

"All right," said Dylan, flexing his muscles. "Stand back . . ."

He moved away from the door and shook his

limbs to warm them up. Dropping his shoulder, he ran full-pelt at the door to knock it down.

"YAAAGGGHHHHH – OWWW!" Dylan yelled, splattering against the door like an egg and sinking to the floor in pain.

"That's a very well-built door," he gasped, his eyes watering as Timmy licked him comfortingly.

"We have to get out of here," Allie announced. "Kids around the world are gonna be brainwashed. We have to do something."

Understandably, Dylan glared at her. Allie was reclining on an inflatable lounge chair, her face covered with a green facial mask and her eyes covered with cucumber slices. Next to her was a tabletop fountain, splashing gently. Wind chimes hung above her, a battery-operated fan blowing them so they tinkled. Her feet were resting in a massage machine, and her open rucksack lay beside her.

"I'd take you more seriously if you weren't in a seaweed wrap," Dylan said through clenched teeth.

"Ha, ha," Allie smirked. "Courtney sent me a spa kit for our anniversary." She switched on the foot massager with her toe and her voice started vibrating. "Y-o-u gotta u-s-e the l-o-o-tion or it goes ba-a-a-d."

"I wonder what they're brainwashing kids to do?" Dylan asked. "Drop out of school? Burn cities?"

A cheery jingle drifted through the heavy, closed door.

"COME ON KIDS," chirped a female voice. "LET'S TAKE THE PLUNGE, JUMP INTO THE RICHNESS OF DEEP-FRIED FUDGE! FUDGIE-FRIES!"

The cucumber slices dropped off Allie's eyes as she sat up straight. "They're making kids spend their money on Fudgie Fries!" she cried. "That's why I'm craving them – we must have been brainwashed yesterday!"

"Yeah," said Dylan. "That's why we felt so weird on the lighthouse – we were being hypnotized!"

Allie shook her head. "If they can make me crave Fudgie Fries, they could make kids do anything. Bad things."

"We have to stop them!" Dylan said, pounding his palm with his fist.

Timmy sniffed around in Allie's open rucksack. He pushed his head into the sack, where he immediately got stuck.

Allie looked down. "Careful, Timmy," she tutted, "that's my spa stuff. I know avocado rub smells good, but it tastes terrible. Believe me on that one."

Timmy gave a muffled growl from deep inside the rucksack. Allie pulled the sack off Timmy's head. To her surprise, Timmy was holding a pair of tweezers in his mouth. He set them down and barked.

"You want to pluck your eyebrows?" said Dylan. "How will you know when to stop?"

Timmy carried the tweezers to the door and hung them on the doorknob. Then he sat down and woofed.

"I see what you're thinking, Timmy!" Allie gasped. "You're an absolute hero!"

"Woof," said Timmy, swaggering a bit and scratching himself enthusiastically.

With her face mask still firmly in place, Allie knelt down by the door and started unscrewing the doorknob with her tweezers.

"Beauty care kits aren't just for glamour," she puffed, twisting the tweezers. "They save lives."

Dylan slid his folded jacket beneath the bottom

of the door and nodded at Allie. She removed the doorknob. With a muffled thunk, the outer doorknob plopped silently on to Dylan's jacket.

Timmy stuck his wet nose into the empty hole and sniffed. Dylan pushed him aside and peered through, studying the cave on the other side.

"They've got a film up on the computer," he said after a minute. Then he snorted with laughter. "Heh-heh! It's a cartoon pelican flying an airplane . . . !"

In the cave, a technician was inserting a CD into a drive. A speaker emitted the high-pitched drone they had heard earlier.

"That's the noise from yesterday," Allie said.

"The one that made us feel so strange," Dylan nodded. He grabbed some cotton wool balls from Allie's spa kit and handed them to his cousin. "Here – quick!"

Already feeling weird, Allie quickly stuffed the cotton wool into her ears. Dylan did the same, after plugging Timmy's ears first. The technician punched a button, muting the drone. Allie and Dylan shook their heads to clear them.

"That was obviously the hypno-frequency," said

Dylan, speaking loudly because of the cotton wool in his ears. "That's what turns you into a zombie! And makes you a Fudgie Fry freak." He stood away from the door, and surveyed the room. "Hmmm," he said thoughtfully. "How can we turn that speaker back on to cover our escape . . . ?"

# Chapter Eight

Dylan's eye fell on the office supplies on the floor. More specifically, on a box of coloured marker pens with interlocking caps and bottoms.

"Got it," said Dylan. "Help me stick those markers together into a long pole, will you?"

Using his mouth, Timmy passed Dylan and Allie the interlocking markers, which they clipped together into a three metre pole. Allie started feeding it through the doorknob hole as Timmy growled encouragement.

"Little to the right," said Dylan, peering through the hole as the markers fed through. "Don't knock over that tea cup . . . All right, you knocked it over, but they didn't see . . . Little further . . ."

The multicoloured marker-pole slowly reached out to the tech-console. Allie gave it a little jab and it pushed a button. The high-pitched drone started humming again.

"Got it!" Dylan said as the technicians in the cave began to slump over their desks into drone-induced trances.

Ten minutes later, Dylan, Allie and Timmy came up out of the trap door into the lighthouse. Allie pulled out her phone.

"Shoot," she said, "no service."

They both turned to the lighthouse door as they heard Kyle's voice approaching.

". . . NOW MY GIRLFRIEND WANTS TO GO DANCING! DO I LOOK LIKE I DANCE?! I DO NOT!"

Kyle would see them if they left through the door. Exchanging glances, Dylan and Allie hurried up the twisting wooden stairs with Timmy close behind. They were all panting by the time they reached the platform at the top. Dylan pounced on an old coil of rope and a cargo net which lay to one side of the platform as Allie pulled out her phone again. She angled it so that the screen caught the sunlight and winked bright.

"I'll signal the pirate ship out there," said Allie, peering out to sea.

"Good idea," said Dylan as he disentangled the rope and net. Then he dropped them so they tangled up again. "The *what?*"

Out on the water, *Queen Anne's Revenge* majestically thrashed through the waves, heading for the island. Max and Jo were at the railing. Max was looking through a telescope at a bright flash coming from the island.

"They're on top of the lighthouse," he said, squinting into the sun.

"Pirate Dan!" Jo called over her shoulder. "Bear north northwest!"

There was a retching sound. Pirate Dan was leaning over the side, being sick.

Jo tutted. "He's seasick, Max," she said. "I'm taking the helm. Stay upwind of Pirate Dan."

A rope and grappling hook whistled down from the

lighthouse platform. The grappling hook snagged on a branch, forming a zip-line from the lighthouse to the ground.

"I learned this from TV," Dylan informed Allie, fixing the cargo net to the zip-line and hoisting a dubious Timmy inside. "And you guys make fun of my deep respect for reality shows! It's sad . . ."

"But it won't work," Allie said as Dylan helped her into the net and climbed in behind her.

"It'll work," Dylan assured her, and pushed off.

The laden net slid down the line towards the tree.

"It'll work, it'll work!" Allie squealed as the net rattled downwards.

The tree limb holding the hook snapped. The rope went limp. Dylan's eyes widened. "It won't work," he said.

They plummeted towards the foliage below. Timmy clambered up Dylan and tried to sit on his head.

"WAAAAAAAAGGGGGHHHH!" Dylan and Allie screamed. "Ooof!"

The net had landed in a stream bed, which ran down the side of the steep bluff. They started sliding rapidly downhill.

"Raooo!" Timmy howled.

"Whee!" yelled Dylan and Allie.

Kyle and his driver had heard Dylan and Allie's screams. They ran to the edge of the bluff, in time to see Dylan, Allie and Timmy hit the beach. Max and Jo were scrambling out of the *Queen*'s motorised dinghy on to the sand. Timmy's howling drifted down the bluff towards them.

"Is that Timmy?" Jo said, wiping her forehead and gazing around.

Timmy rocketed out of the bottom of the stream bed and flew into Max, flattening him.

"Yes," said Max, in a smothered voice.

Allie and Dylan shot out of the stream bed and landed on Jo.

"Dylan and Allie, too," Jo spluttered.

Moments later, the kids lashed the motorised dinghy to the stern of the *Queen* and pushed Timmy aboard, climbing up after him.

"No more waves," Pirate Dan mumbled, curled up on the deck and sounding weak. "No more water . . ."

"We have to sail this thing ourselves," Jo said. "Max – hoist the jib, Allie – belay starboard tackle. Dylan – shake a reef in the foretop!"

There was a pause as Jo wondered if her cousins had understood a single word. Then . . .

"Aye-aye, Jo!" Max, Dylan and Allie shouted.

# Chapter Nine

Max, Allie and Dylan scampered around the deck of the *Queen Anne's Revenge* to do the chores Jo had outlined, coiling rope, expertly making knots and hoisting canvas.

The ship moved to life.

But roaring round the corner towards them came a 15-metre powerboat, driven by Kyle and crawling with his henchmen. They were blocking the mouth of the cove. There was no way past!

"Woof," Timmy barked. "Woof woof!"

"You're right, Timmy," Jo gasped as the powerboat approached. "We're trapped. These jokers are starting to make me mad." She put the helm hard over, trying to manoeuvre round. But the powerboat easily cut them off again, before coming alongside.

"AHOY, *QUEEN ANNE'S REVENGE!*" Kyle yelled triumphantly over the roar of the engine. "SURRENDER AND MEET YOUR DOOM!"

Max ran to a cupboard and opened up the ship's first-aid kit. He pulled out a length of rubber tubing. Then he lashed the surgical tubing between two belaying pins, creating a catapult.

"Not today, Angry Dude . . ." Max puffed.

"I see what you're doing," said Dylan, running up to join his cousin. "Pirate Dan," he called, "do you have any cannonballs?"

Pirate Dan coughed and staggered to his feet. "Too expensive," he mumbled.

"We need something heavy," said Dylan, thinking fast.

"There's a two kilo sack of flour in the galley," Pirate Dan said, clutching his stomach gingerly. "But I *was* going to make a victoria sponge . . ."

Timmy emerged from below deck with the heavy sack of flour in his mouth. He set it down and pushed it with his nose. It slid across the ship, landing neatly in the middle of a shuffleboard target painted on the deck.

"Here it is," said Allie, handing the sack to Max as Timmy made pleased woofing sounds. "Aim for the windscreen."

As Dylan rigged another catapult, Max shot the flour at the powerboat. It hit the windscreen and exploded in a huge cloud, blinding Kyle who coughed and swerved the boat, causing a few henchmen to fall overboard.

"Get up front and clean the screen!" Kyle screamed at a crewman through a mouthful of flour.

As the crewman made his way forward, Dylan handed Max the second catapult and a balloon filled with liquid.

"This is no time for a water-balloon fight," said Max, wagging his finger at Dylan.

Dylan grinned. "It's cooking oil."

"Cool!" Max cried.

He loaded the oil-balloon into the catapult and fired it at the powerboat.

SPLAT!

The oil splattered all over the foredeck. The henchman cleaning the windscreen slipped, windmilled his arms wildly and plummeted overboard.

"Hey, Dylan!" Max yelled. "You're missing some ace footage!"

Dylan tapped his hat. The camera that was strapped to his hat wobbled a little but stayed in place. "Got it all up here," he said. He handed Max another balloon. "Here," he said. "It's full of paint!"

The henchman who had fallen overboard suddenly popped his head over the side of the *Queen* with an evil grin, having scrambled up the *Queen's* ladder. Swinging around to him, Allie pulled a face.

The effect of the green face mask still covering her was startling.

"Boogie boogie!" she yelled.

"Aaaggghhhh!" shrieked the henchman, letting go of the ladder and falling back into the sea.

Pleased, Allie wiped the mask off her face. "Beauty products," she said in a satisfied voice. "There's nothing they can't do."

SPLAT!

Dylan's paint balloon struck the windscreen of the powerboat. Briefly, it drifted away from the *Queen*.

"But we can't get away from them!" Jo cried, struggling to steer the *Queen Anne's Revenge* clear.

"Flip over the chart table," Pirate Dan coughed, clinging on to the main mast.

Timmy leaped into the air and landed on the edge of the wooden desk behind the ship's wheel. The top flipped over, tossing Timmy to the deck and revealing a high-tech console, complete with GPS, ship-to-shore and numerous control buttons. Suddenly, it was clear that the *Queen Anne's Revenge* had a valuable secret up her sleeve!

# Chapter Ten

The cousins gawped at the state-of-the-art control panel.

"She's got twin 1200-horsepower fuel-injected engines," said Pirate Dan.

Jo grinned with delight. "I can work with that . . ." she murmured.

Pressing a button, she fired up the engines. The *Queen* shivered for an instant, then rocketed away in a plume of white water.

"YOU ARE NOT GETTING AWAY!" Kyle screamed, jumping up and down with rage and shaking his paint-covered fists at the *Queen*. Leaping down into the driving seat, he revved the powerboat's engine and gave chase.

"Want to bet?" Jo said.

She put the helm hard over. The *Queen* roared around until she was facing the powerboat.

"There's a time for manoeuvring, and a time to play 'chicken'," Jo grinned as the others cheered. "It's chicken time!"

She gunned the throttle. The *Queen* rocketed towards Kyle.

"DO I HAVE MORE NERVE THAN YOU?" Kyle yelled, gunning his own throttle and heading towards the *Queen*. The *Queen* showed no sign of changing direction. Kyle panicked. "I DO NOT!"

He turned hard. The powerboat crashed into the rocky point jutting out from Shelter Island. The entire crew of bad guys was hurled from the boat. One flew through the air and landed in a tree on shore, where a pelican perched on him. Another emerged from the sea, sputtering, his face covered with pinching crabs. The powerboat took on water and started to sink.

"Guys," Dylan said, grabbing the ship-to-shore radio, "would now be a good time to call the police?"

"Hang on just a sec . . ." said Allie, placing a case

of Fudgie Fries in the sling. She fired it at Kyle, who was scrambling out of the water on the rocky point. It hit him in the back of the head and brought him down.

"Fudgie Fries are *not* good for you," Allie grinned.

Half an hour later, two police boats with flashing lights were at the wooden dock on the mainland. The kids, Timmy and George watched as a stout, stern-looking police constable loaded a handcuffed Kyle on to a boat which was already filled with other henchmen. Following him aboard was a queasy Pirate Dan on a stretcher.

Allie pulled a tiny card from her pocket and scribbled on it.

*Dear Courtney, here's a souvenir of my latest adventure. On a pirate ship, no less! I hope you like it.*

Then she stuck the note to a huge boat anchor.

"Could you deliver this to my friend Courtney?" Allie asked, turning to the glum-looking postman standing beside her. "Her address is on the card."

The postman sighed and shouldered the anchor. "I should've been a librarian," he muttered as he loaded the anchor into his tiny rowing boat and rowed away.

The stout, stern police constable approached them.

"We've seized all the bootleggers' equipment," said Constable Lily Stubblefield. "There'll be no more brainwashing round here. Good job, you kids – maybe you'll grow up to join the police force."

"My future's right here," Dylan grinned, holding up his DVD camera. "Somebody will pay a fortune for this footage."

"Very likely," said Constable Stubblefield, before taking the disc. "Unfortunately, we have to confiscate it as evidence. You'll get it back when the trial's over."

"What?" Dylan said in horror. "Well, how long will that take?"

Constable Stubblefield shrugged. "These days? No more than three, four years, tops. Cheerio."

She walked back to her troops.

"Four years?" Dylan groaned. "I can't wait that long to be rich!"

"You kids should be proud," George said, putting her arm around Jo's shoulders. "You worked together as a team. You . . ." She noticed a strange-looking plant growing nearby. "Ooh, a Creeping Fernelius!" she said in excitement. "The poison in those will turn your brain into mushy peas! Who wants to help harvest it?"

Jo carefully removed her mother's arm from around her shoulders. "We'd love to!" she said. "But, um . . . we've got to go!"

And the cousins scarpered across to the *Queen Anne's Revenge*, with Timmy the dog racing beside them. Leaping aboard first, Timmy pressed the starter button. The engines roared to life just as the kids jumped aboard. The boat hydroplaned across the waves, leaping out of the water as everyone stood in the prow and relished the seaspray.

"Woof woof!" Timmy barked from the helm.

"WHOO!" shouted the cousins, punching the air in unison.

# Epilogue

Steadying himself against the mast of Jo's boat, Dylan peered through his viewfinder at Jo. The little boat was bouncing through the waves. Allie was nearby, looking queasy.

"Okay," Dylan said to Jo, "we're rolling. A Sticky Situation, Number 62. Action, Jo."

"The water's quite choppy today," Jo announced. She started making swooping motions with her arms. "The waves are going UP and DOWN and WAA-AAY UP and WAA-AY DOWN . . ."

"Stop," said Allie weakly. "I get it. It's choppy."

"Oh, are you feeling a little seasick?" said Jo in surprise. "If you ever get seasick, move to the middle of the boat – there's less motion from the waves there."

Allie tottered to the middle of the boat.

"Make sure you get plenty of fresh air . . ." Jo continued.

Allie breathed deeply and nodded. "What's next?"

"Face the direction the boat's going, and focus on an unmoving object in the distance," Jo instructed.

Allie swallowed and pointed ashore. "How 'bout that tree?" she asked, focusing intently. Her brow cleared. "I think it's working!" she said. "I feel better. I feel calmer."

A seagull fluttered down landed on the rail near Allie. Still focusing hard on the shore, Allie didn't notice. The seagull lazily scratched itself, before opening its large yellow beak.

"SQUAAAWWWWWK!"

"Waaagh!" said Allie, leaping out of her skin and falling overboard.

SPLOOSH!

"Of course," Jo added, tossing a lifebelt towards Allie and pulling her cousin back to the boat, "staying in the boat is very important, too."

"You falling in was great!" said Dylan eagerly,

peering around from the edge of his viewfinder. "Let's get it from another angle . . . !"

## LOOK OUT FOR THE WHOLE SERIES!

# THE CASE OF THE PLANT
# THAT COULD EAT YOUR HOUSE

**Hodder
Children's
Books**

A division of Hachette Children's Books

## Special thanks to Lucy Courtenay and Artful Doodlers

A Catalogue record for this book is available from the British Library

ISBN 978 0 340 95977 0

Typeset in Weiss by Avon DataSet Ltd,
Bidford on Avon, Warwickshire

Printed in Great Britain by
Clays Ltd, St Ives plc

The paper and board used in this paperback by Hodder Children's
Books are natural recyclable products made from wood grown in
sustainable forests. The manufacturing processes conform to the
environmental regulations of the country of origin.

Hodder Children's Books
a division of Hachette Children's Books
338 Euston Road, London NW1 3BH
An Hachette Livre UK Company
www.hachettelivre.co.uk

# Chapter One

In the cold moonlight, two dark figures crept towards the large greenhouse. Listening intently for danger, they pulled their coat collars up and adjusted the brims of their hats so that their faces couldn't be seen. They moved closer, until they were almost at the greenhouse door.

SNAP!

One of the figures hopped in silent pain, clutching his foot. A large mousetrap was attached to his toe. The second figure studied the greenhouse door and rattled it hopefully. It was locked. Pulling a nail file from an inside pocket, the second figure tried to jimmy the lock – with no luck.

1

The sound of singing made both figures jump.

"ROW, ROW, ROW YOUR KAYAK, GENTLY DOWN THE STREAM," boomed a boy's voice.

"A TWIG FELL INTO ALLIE'S KAYAK AND SHE LET OUT A SCREAM!" chirped a second boy.

A dog barked in what sounded like agreement. "Woof!"

"It looked like a snake!" complained a girl's voice.

The figures looked at each other. There was no time to lose. The first figure snatched up a rock and smashed a panel of glass next to the greenhouse door handle. The other reached in and unlocked the door. They both slipped inside, vanishing into the shadows.

Several metres from the greenhouse, Max, Dylan, Allie, and Jo trooped towards Jo's house. They were each carrying a kayak upside down on their heads and Timmy the dog followed them.

"Sure," Dylan scoffed, his voice echoing inside his kayak. "A snake with leaves!" He suddenly stopped and pointed at the ground. "Look, another one!" he gasped. Then: "Oh no, it's, a twig. Ha!"

"Ha, ha – funny!" said Allie, flicking her long blond hair. The movement jerked her head

2

sideways, making her kayak clonk against the kayak on Dylan's head.

"G'uh," said Dylan, losing his balance and staggering smack into the trunk of a nearby apple tree. The tree showered apples on him, burying Dylan in a huge pile until just the tip of his kayak could be seen.

"Thanks, Dylan," Jo laughed, hefting her kayak down and laying it beside the back door of the house. She tucked her brown hair behind her ears. "Now I don't have to pick those apples."

Timmy took an apple in his mouth as Allie and Max dumped their kayaks beside Jo's and disappeared inside the house, leaving Dylan behind.

"Wait for me!" Dylan cried, struggling out of the apples. Straightening his glasses, he hurried after his cousins.

The coast was clear. The two figures watching from the greenhouse sidled out of the door, their arms laden with potted plants, and scurried away into the darkness.

"Aunt George!" Allie cried as the cousins all clattered into the house. "We're back!"

"And we're hungry," Max added, peering around from beneath his blond fringe. "Ve-rrry hungry!"

Dylan noticed some newspaper on the floor in a corner of the cosy living room. On the newspaper was a puddle of oil, some greasy bolts, a couple of nuts and a spanner.

"Looks like Aunt George is house-training a robot," Dylan joked.

"Dad's re-building a carburettor," Jo explained. "They went to the antique car show over in Stilton. They won't be back till tomorrow."

"Looks like we're on our own," Dylan said, rubbing his hands. "Allie? You can make us some fruit smoothies."

"You can help," Allie said firmly, seizing Dylan by his shirt collar and dragging him with her into the kitchen.

"Hoimp!" Dylan protested, scrabbling his feet uselessly on the floor as Allie towed him away. Jo, Max and Timmy followed.

Rolling up her sleeves, Allie marched across to the blender and took off the lid.

"Banana!" she ordered over her shoulder.

Dylan took a banana from the fruit bowl and

4

peeled it. Then he tossed it towards the ceiling fan. *Slice! Slice! Slice!* went the fan, chopping the banana into neat pieces. Allie held out the blender jug and caught them as they fell.

Max pulled open the fridge and grabbed a coconut, before tossing it to Jo. Jo dribbled the coconut expertly around the kitchen, bobbing it neatly on her knees and feet. Then she gave it a swift, hard kick. The coconut rocketed through the air towards a large suit of armour standing by the

back door, where it impaled itself on a spike sticking out of the suit's armoured helmet. As the coconut milk streamed out, Timmy pushed a cup with his nose so it moved under the milk and caught it. He then pushed the cup towards Allie.

"Teamwork," grinned Allie. "Nothing like it."

Outside, the two dark figures carried more armloads of plants to a nearby horse-drawn wagon, which they had parked well away from the house. With particular care, they placed a tall, bamboo-like plant in the very back. The plant's tendrils waved menacingly in the darkness. They looked like fingers reaching for a victim's throat.

Standing next to the blender in the kitchen, Allie dropped in a strawberry with a satisfied look on her face. "Strawberry," she announced. "The last step in Allie's Scrumptious Super Smoothies."

She turned on the blender button. Timmy leaped for cover under the kitchen table as pink smoothie sprayed everywhere. Jo, Max and Dylan covered their heads with their arms as the smoothie splattered them from head to foot.

"Maybe the last step should be 'putting the lid on'," Jo advised, lowering her arms.

"I never do that back home," said Allie, staring at the mess in surprise. Then she brightened. "Maybe it's the time change."

"Too bad you're not making these smoothies at Blaine and Daine Dunston's 'exclusive' party," said Dylan, fetching some kitchen towel as Max wiped a fingerful of smoothie off his face and sampled it. "I could clean up on cleaning up." He put on a loud vendor's voice. "Paper towels, one pound each! Three for five pounds!"

Dylan handed Max a paper towel, then held out his hand for payment.

"Cheers," said Max, absently shaking Dylan's hand with a sticky squelch.

"Everyone in the village keeps yabbering on about the Dunstons' party," Jo groaned. "I don't want to hear another word about it."

"I hear they're going to have Prince Philip do magic tricks," said Allie eagerly, "and then there's—"

Jo put her hands over her ears. "I'm not listening!!!"

As Max wiped more smoothie off his arm, Allie

suddenly said: "Hey, Max, what's that bruise on your arm?"

Max studied the discolouration on his forearm and shrugged. "Probably just something I got kayaking," he said.

Dylan, still annoyed with Max for squelching his hand, got a mischievous look on his face. "Or is it?" he said, before adding in a melodramatic voice: "What if it's . . . beri-beri?"

Max looked uneasy. "What . . . ? Nah . . . Yeah? Nah . . ."

Dylan wagged a finger at his cousin. "You're always talking about secret government experiments," he continued. "Who knows what they put in your drinking water?"

Dylan picked up the *Family Medical Encyclopedia* from some books on the kitchen counter and leafed through it. "Let's see," he said seriously. "Has your heart-rate been elevated lately?"

Max snatched the book and studied it with an anxious look on his face.

"Of course it has," Jo pointed out, wringing out Timmy's smoothie-sodden tail into a bucket. "He's been kayaking all day."

"That thing on his arm isn't beri-beri," Allie said. "It's berry-smoothie." Pleased with herself, she laughed. "That was a good one! I didn't have that prepared, or anything."

Max peered more closely at the book with a horrorstruck expression on his face. "One of the symptoms is partial paralysis," he said. "I could get numb-neck!" He let his head flop down sideways until it rested on his shoulder. "See?" he wailed. "Numb-neck!"

Suddenly, there was a loud noise outside.

CCRRASSHH!

# Chapter Two

The Five rushed outside, to see the broken remains of a potted plant on the ground. Two dark figures were scrambling into their horse-drawn wagon and picking up the reins.

"Hey!" Jo shouted, noticing the waving leaves of a dozen plants in the back of the wagon. "Stop! Those are my mum's!"

One of the figures snapped the reins. His horse reared and broke into a run, pulling the wagon behind him. The thieves were getting away!

"After them!" Jo shouted, running for her bike.

The others did the same. Leaping astride and pedalling like fury, the Five gave chase with Timmy

10

barking madly beside them.

The horse-drawn wagon swerved and thundered down a small country lane. In hot pursuit, the cousins raced along the dark road on their bikes, lights bobbing as they chased the thundering wagon.

"Turn here," Jo yelled as the wagon disappeared around a corner. "Shortcut!"

She led them off the road and they started down a steep, thickly wooded slope. As they slalomed through the dense stand of trees, Allie called out warnings about the obstacles in their path.

"Tree! Tree! Tree! Tree! Tree! Tree! Tree! . . . Hedgehog!"

Sure enough, a hedgehog had waddled into the gleam of the headlights. Automatically swerving to avoid it, the cousins disappeared into a leafy hedge looming in their path.

"Ow! . . ." they yelled, bouncing through leaves and twigs with Timmy in hot pursuit. "Youch! . . . Oof! . . . Pfuh!" They exploded from the hedge trailing leaves and branches, spluttering but still riding fast.

At the foot of the slope, the wagon sped along a

road toward a rickety wooden bridge over a swift stream. The kids flew down on to the road, pedalling furiously.

The bridge wasn't strong enough to take the weight of a speeding wagon. It creaked and groaned as the wagon raced over it, then cracked and began to give way just as the wagon reached the far side.

BOOOM!

The bridge collapsed just as the Five approached it.

Max's eyes landed on a slanting tree growing out over the river.

"Going up!" Max cried, twisting his wheels and speeding up the tree before leaping into the air and landing safely on the other side of the stream.

"Here goes Jo!" Jo shouted, following close behind.

"Allie-oop!" Allie squealed, leaping higher than either Max or Jo as she flew over the stream gorge.

"I can't think of anything clever!" Dylan bellowed, jumping the gorge as Timmy plunged into the stream and swam across.

They were gaining on the wagon.

"We're going to catch 'em!" Max shouted.

*EEEEEEEEE!*

They were interrupted by a train whistle. The wagon was racing towards a train crossing as a long freight train approached.

"We're not going to catch 'em," Dylan said, shaking his head.

The wagon narrowly squeaked in front of the train engine. As it did so, its wheels bumped on the tracks and a VHS tape flew out of the back. It soared through the air and landed on a rock, breaking apart. The spool of tape clattered out of the broken housing, and the tape unravelled in the air.

Screeching to a halt, the Five watched helplessly as the train lumbered by. When the last carriage had thundered past, the wagon had vanished from sight.

Jo jumped off her bike and picked up the VHS tape. "They left a souvenir," she said, waving the tape. "And maybe a clue!"

"I'd rather they left me money for my trouble," Dylan grumbled. "Who has VHS any more?"

Out of sight, the horse-drawn wagon plodded

on along a narrow lane through the forest. A small tendril was forcing its way out of the tall, bamboo-like plant in the back. It waved lazily, almost as if it was sniffing the air.

Back at Jo's place, the kids shone their torches into the looted greenhouse. A few wilted plants remained, amongst upturned potting benches, scattered bags of plant food and mounds of scattered compost.

Allie whistled. "Whooo!! It looks like my favourite boutique after a half-price sale."

"It'll take some time to fix this," said Jo, holding up the tape, "but maybe it can tell us who we're looking for."

Max sneezed violently. "I think I've got it!" he said.

Allie swung round to her cousin. "You know who stole the plants?" she said in excitement.

Max wielded the *Family Medical Encyclopedia*. "No, I think I've got Kretchlow's Disease. Symptoms are sneezing, fatigue, watery eyes . . ."

"You're probably just allergic to one of the plants that was in here," Jo interrupted.

"It could be that . . ." Max thrust the book at Jo.

"Or it could be Greenblatt's Syndrome! I could grow hair on my eyes!"

"Before you do, take a look at this," said Dylan, kneeling by the greenhouse door handle and studying it.

"Someone tried to jimmy it!" Allie gasped, looking over Dylan's shoulder. "Like the lock on the back gate at school that you have to force if you want to sneak out at lunch and get a pedicure."

Max, Dylan and Jo stared at Allie. Timmy gave a disapproving whine.

"Not that I've ever done that," Allie said hastily.

Jo pointed at the ground. "Now these metal flakes on the ground must be from the thieves trying to open the lock."

"But who would—" Max began, before breaking off with an enormous sneeze. "Ah-choo! . . . AH-CHOO! . . . WAHHH-CH-SCHPMOOO!"

"Max makes a good point," Dylan said. "Who would want to go to all this trouble to steal a bunch of boring plants?"

Jo frowned. "My mum grows some pretty strange plants. Whatever the thieves were after, it's not boring . . ."

Safely locked in an old garden shed several miles away, the strange bamboo-like plant was getting taller. Tendrils were unfurling like baby tentacles. A root cracked its way through the ceramic pot holding the plant and began to crawl menacingly across the dirt floor.

# Chapter Three

The following morning, the Five gathered in the study. Max was still in his dressing gown, and sat on the sofa clutching the *Family Medical Encyclopedia* with a box of tissues by his side.

An old, hand-cranked gramophone stood on the desk. Jo placed an empty spool of thread on to the turntable, than fitted the plastic spool of a video cassette tape over the top. Nearby, Allie stood with the bare brown videotape wrapped around her arms like knitting wool.

Dylan seized the gramophone handle and began to crank it. To the tinny tune of *God Save the Queen*, the videotape wound rapidly and tidily on to the

plastic spool. When it was done, Jo popped the whole thing back into its plastic casing.

"Let's see if this tells us anything about the thieves," she said, hurrying over to the VCR and putting in the mended tape.

The TV flickered to life. The picture showed the greenhouse. A young chimpanzee in a blazer bearing the FGTV logo was sitting on George's head, clutching her face with his feet.

"It tells us one of them wears a nappy and sits on your mum's head," Dylan said.

The picture widened to show a young TV reporter standing beside George.

"This is your on-the-spot reporter, Polly Lucas, with local botanist George Kirrin Misra," said the reporter brightly.

The chimp screeched.

"And, as always, Prince Extremely Hairy, the FGTV newschimp," Polly Lucas added, sounding a little less bright.

The chimp leaped from George's head on to a vine hanging down from the greenhouse roof. He swung in a loop and patted his head derisively, before pursing his rubbery lips and blowing a raspberry.

"So," Polly Lucas said, in a determined I'm-going-to-ignore-the-chimp voice, "your new plant. Tell us about it."

George picked up a bamboo-like plant as Prince Extremely Hairy swung past. "It's a hybrid of two very fast-growing plants, kudzu and bamboo," George said, stroking the leaves fondly. "I call it 'Bambuzu'." She ducked as a banana skin flew through the air. "Incoming!" she shouted.

The chimp screeched with laughter as the banana skin landed on Polly's head.

"In terrain ravaged by fire, or islands after storms, bambuzu can quickly re-grow damaged areas and preserve the land," George continued.

Polly pulled the banana skin off her head with a sour expression on her face. "You could probably make a fortune if it grows as you say it does," she said.

"Yes," George said eagerly, "but I'm more interested in the environmental . . . Oh, dear – tomato blitz!"

The chimp had plucked a tomato off a plant and hurled it towards George and Polly. They dodged the pulpy missile, which smashed straight into the

camera lens and turned the picture red.

"Are you guys thinking what I'm thinking?" said Jo as the image blurred to electronic snow.

"Absolutely," said Dylan enthusiastically. "That chimp's a gold mine. He should have his own show!"

"If Aunt George's bambuzu plant is so valuable," Allie said, ignoring Dylan, "that's probably what the thieves were after."

Jo turned off the video. "Exactly," she said. "Let's go straight to the police station – we'll tell Constable Stubblefield what we know and she can get my mum's plants back."

From the sofa, Max said in a feeble voice: "You'd better go without me. I've been reading the medical guide all night and I think I'm coming down with chronic sleeping syndrome – it makes you really tired." He stood up and hobbled towards the stairs.

"So does staying up all night reading medical guides," Jo sighed. "See what you've done, Dylan? He thinks he's got everything in that silly book."

Max dragged himself slowly up a few steps.

"But MAX is fearless," said Allie in surprise. "He never worried about getting sick before."

20

Max had already given up the climb, and had curled up on the stairs for a nap.

"Oh, it's not fear, it's imagination," Jo said. "He'll snap out of it soon."

They all turned at the sound of snoring. Max had fallen asleep, and was now sliding down the stairs and bumping his chin on every step.

"Hmmm, poor guy," Allie said, sounding worried. "Even if he is imagining it, he needs somebody to look after him. I don't mind not going to the police station – nothing ever happens there, anyway."

Jo, Dylan and Timmy walked down to Falcongate. As they reached the police station, the front door burst open and a weedy-looking thief fled through the door, pursued by Constable Lily Stubblefield. As they watched, Constable Stubblefield hurtled through the air and tackled the thief, bringing him down at Jo, Timmy and Dylan's feet. Constable Stubblefield got up, puffing a bit and holding tightly on to the struggling villain.

"Constable Stubblefield," said Jo, "we want to report a break-in."

"I hope it wasn't at the Dunston house," said Constable Stubblefield, marching the wriggling thief up the steps of the police station. "That would ruin their magnificent party. I hear they're having a 10-metre chocolate waterfall."

"As Prime Minister Winston Churchill once said," Jo said in a low voice to Dylan, "Whoop-de-stinking-do!"

Constable Stubblefield dragged the thief inside the station. Jo, Dylan and Timmy followed close behind.

"Anyhow . . ." Jo continued, "as I was saying . . . the break-in was at our house."

"Let me get Fingers Mulrooney here sorted out, and I'll take your report," Constable Stubblefield said over her shoulder. She pushed Fingers Mulrooney into a chair. "Sit there, you," she told him. Then she picked up a pencil and looked enquiringly at Jo and Dylan.

"Aunt George has grown a valuable plant called bambuzu," Dylan began. "We think the thieves were after it."

As Constable Stubblefield wrote this down, Fingers snuck out of his chair and tip-toed towards

an open window. He began to climb out.

"Don't worry, you kids," said Constable Stubblefield, making a note on her pad.

Without looking up, she picked up a heavy book and hurled it at the window. The jolt caused the heavy window to slide down on top of Fingers, pinning him helplessly to the window frame.

"Constable Lily Stubblefield is on the job," said Constable Stubblefield. "I won't rest until I find the culprits." She glanced at her watch. Her expression changed. "Hello! It's lunchtime."

She produced a sandwich and a girlie fashion magazine from her desk drawer. Then, as Dylan and Jo exchanged exasperated looks, she started chewing her sandwich carefully and deliberately.

# Chapter Four

Max sat on the edge of his bed, soaking his feet in hot water. A thermometer was in his mouth and an ice-bag was on his head. Taking his blood pressure with one hand, he covered his eye with the other as he studied an eye chart on the wall.

"Bad news," said Max in a hollow voice as Allie came in, carrying food on a tray. "I'm getting snow blindness." He gave an enormous sneeze that almost lifted him out of the bed. "And it makes me sneeze," he snuffled.

"Here you go," Allie said as she set the tray on Max's lap. "Vaporizers, air purifier, thermal wraps, sitz bath solution, ear-drops, eye-drops, nose-drops . . ."

24

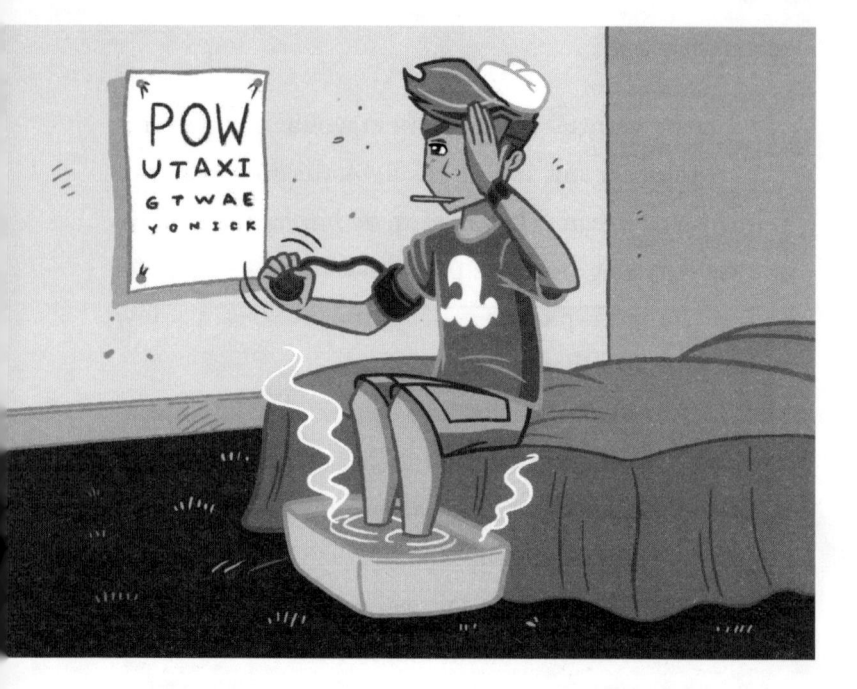

Max looked down at the tray. The ice-bag fell off his head into a bowl of soup, which splashed all over Allie.

"And chicken soup," Allie finished crossly, "which by the way took me a very long time to make."

Max gave another huge sneeze, sending the medical supplies on the tray flying.

"I guess chicken soup makes me sneeze, too," he sniffed, thumbing through the *Family Medical Encyclopedia*. "Let's see . . . chickens . . ."

                              *  *  *

"Maybe Constable Stubblefield would come over if
we told her our house has a Matterhorn made of
whipped cream," Dylan said, as he, Jo and Timmy
walked away from the police station in Falcongate.
He stopped, picturing it. "Whipped cream! How
great would that be?"

   "I'm not waiting for her," Jo said, striding ahead
with Timmy beside her. "These are my mum's
plants, and I want them back. What would you do
if you'd stolen bambuzu?"

   Dylan shrugged. "Same as I'd do in any situation.
Try to get filthy, stinkin', stupid rich."

   "Of course!" Jo exclaimed. "Follow me!"


Half an hour later, Jo, Dylan and Timmy stepped
out of the plant nursery with Mr Tyler, the nursery
owner. Mr Tyler was shaking his head.

   "Sorry, kids. No one's tried to sell me any exotic
or valuable plants."

   "So no unusual activity at all?" Jo said hopefully.

   Mr Tyler scratched his nose. "Just the Dunstons
buying every flower I've got for their big party. I
hear they're going to have an astronaut who walked

on the moon to make balloon-animals."

A snooty-sounding voice made Jo and Dylan turn round.

"The Kirrins aren't invited to our party," said Blaine Dunston, who was leaning against the wall on the far side of the street. At his feet was a huge pile of canned drinks, bags of candy, party supplies and, teetering on the very top, a life-sized ice sculpture of Blaine and his twin sister Daine.

Standing beside Blaine, Daine giggled and dabbed face glitter on to her face. "Our party is only for our kind of people," she sneered.

"Oh, you mean, rats who have learned to walk upright?" Dylan shot back.

Before Blaine and Daine could think of an answer, an old, rattletrap pick-up truck wheezed up to the curb and groaned to a halt. A shabby, mild old fellow in gardening overalls got out.

Daine put her face glitter in her teensy little purse. "You're five minutes late, Crawford!" she snapped. "We can tell our father to get a new groundsman, you know!"

Without looking at the twins, Crawford hefted the ice sculpture on to his back. Jo and Dylan

gasped as he staggered under its weight and slipped over. The ice statue fell on top of him and pinned him to the pavement.

"Careful, Crawford," Blaine drawled. He didn't move an inch to help the old man to his feet. "Don't you dare hurt that sculpture!"

Jo had had enough. "You two blisters think just because your father's rich, you can order anyone around," she blazed. "That you're better than everyone."

"We're better than you," said Blaine as Crawford struggled to his feet. "I can do *anything* better than you."

"Oh, really?" Jo snarled, starting forward. "Like what?"

Blaine glanced lazily up and down the street. "Like, I bet I can swing farther than you on that rope, Miss I'm-So-Athletic," he said. He pointed to a rope hanging from a block-and-tackle that was secured to a cleat on the wall of Mr Tyler's plant nursery.

"I could beat you in my sleep," Jo said, rolling up her sleeves.

Dylan stared and Timmy put his head under his

28

paws as Jo grabbed the rope end, climbed up on to the bonnet of Crawford's truck and then hopped up to the roof. She took a swing and leaped off the truck, swinging out over the street.

Daine sneaked over to the knot which secured the rope to the wall-cleat and loosened it just as Jo was at the point of swinging back again. With a slithering sound, the rope paid out of the block-and-tackle. Jo fell in a heap, right into a muddy puddle in the road.

"Ha!" Blaine sniggered as Jo blinked the mud out of her eyes and Dylan and Timmy rushed out to help her up. "Maybe you *should* try it in your sleep next time!"

# Chapter Five

Back at Jo's house later that morning, Dylan and Jo walked slowly up the drive with Timmy close behind. Jo was still wiping mud off her face with her handkerchief.

"You missed a spot," said Dylan as Jo put the handkerchief back in her pocket, adding helpfully: ". . . all over your body."

They swung around the corner. An antique car was parked outside the front door. It was rusty, and several pieces of the engine lay on the drive beside it. A pair of tweed trouser-clad legs stuck out from beneath the car.

The thunderous expression on Jo's face cleared.

"My parents are back!" she said eagerly, and hurried over to the legs. "Dad, did you hear what happened?" she said, bending down to peer underneath the car.

"About the break-in?" said the tweed legs in a strong Indian accent. "Indeed. Very unfortunate. But I found the carburettor I needed, which is jolly good news!"

Jo glanced up as George came out of the house, carrying a potted geranium and a glass of water. She looked upset.

"Don't worry, Mum," Jo said at once. "We're going to find your plants."

George set the geranium carefully down on the drive. "I hope so," she said sadly. "Max and Allie told me what happened. I agree with your theory that the thieves were after my bambuzu."

Jo's dad Ravi slid out from underneath the car. "Pardon me, dear – did you bring my water?" he said to George.

"I did," said George, holding up the glass. "Do you mind if Ophelia has a little? She's quite upset by all the fuss."

George poured most of the water over the

geranium before handing Ravi the glass. Ravi drank the few drops that were left.

"Strangely," he said in a resigned voice, "I'm still thirsty."

"Speaking of water," said George thoughtfully, "I hope the bambuzu doesn't get too much. It's meant for arid regions – too much water will make it spread faster than pimples on a teenager's forehead."

Images of a hot summer's day came into Jo's head. In her mind's eye, she saw people tossing beach balls back and forth as a tidal-wave of bambuzu swarmed over the beach.

"And there's no stopping it once it's established," George continued.

The tidal wave of bambuzu in Jo's head began engulfing the sun-bathers and wrapping around the beach-ball players, its tendrils dragging them down and then popping the beach balls for good measure. She exchanged worried glances with Dylan.

"It could spread all over the world," George was saying.

Now it was Dylan's turn to imagine the havoc that the bambuzu might wreak. He pictured the Eiffel Tower with bambuzu tendrils shooting up its

iron sides and pulling it down with a mighty clang on top of hundreds of startled tourists.

"I hate to think what could happen," George finished sadly.

Now Dylan's imagination was in New York. The tendrils of bambuzu were swirling up the Statue of Liberty, pulling off her dress and leaving her in her underwear. Dylan's mind went into overdrive as he pictured Liberty leaping into the water and swimming for her life with the bambuzu in hot pursuit.

"Well, we'll just have to find that bambuzu fast," said Allie firmly.

She and Max had come out of the house just in time to hear George's words of doom.

"And hope it doesn't get too much water," Max added, wrapping himself more tightly into his dressing gown.

BRA-DA-BOOOM!

The sky gave an ominous rumble. Clouds suddenly blotted out the sun. Everything grew cold and quiet, before a brilliant flash of lightning tore overhead and the rain began tipping down.

Ravi hurriedly threw a sheet over his antique car,

and he and George dashed inside. The Five
followed, exchanging worried looks. If the
bambuzu grew as quickly when it got wet as
George said, they were in *big* trouble.

In the old garden shed several miles away, the roof
had sprung a leak. Water streamed through the
hole, straight on to the bambuzu plant. Almost
immediately, the bambuzu began to grow faster
than ever. Tendrils shot out in every direction.
Roots shattered through the pot and dived into the
ground. The tendrils grew until they pushed up
against the shed walls. Undeterred, they punched
their way out through the wood, shattered the
shed's dingy windows and took off into the rain.

# Chapter Six

The following morning, there was no sign of the previous day's torrential downpour. The sun blazed down on the green fields and hedges that looped around the small town of Falcongate. Birds sang in the trees, and in a meadow on the outskirts of the town a tinny loudspeaker played odd marching music and a large banner proclaimed: "FALCONGATE JUMBLE SALE!"

In the meadow, dozens of merchants had set up tables to sell a motley assortment of wares: toys, books, furniture, blenders and books.

The Five wandered up to the five-bar gate that marked the entrance to the meadow, and felt

around in their pockets for some entrance money.

"Glad you're feeling better Max," said Allie pulling out a few coins and paying the gate attendant.

Max felt his pulse. "I was pretty sure I had Dutch elm disease," he said seriously, "but I guess it was the twenty-four hour kind."

Dylan pocketed his change and stared around the large meadow. It was buzzing with noise and activity. "So, Jo," he said, "do you really think there are people selling stolen goods here?"

"Well there are *some* honest merchants," said Jo, "but lots of people sell bootleg music, counterfeit clothes . . ."

Timmy growled warily, pricking up his ears and glancing from side to side.

"Now don't let your guard down for a minute," Jo warned, patting Timmy. "This place is crawling with ruthless, dangerous cut-throats."

A sweet old lady limped towards the Five, holding out a plate of something. "Would you like some tea-cakes?" she quavered.

"OK, maybe not her," Jo conceded as the old lady moved on. "But I bet someone around here has

heard or seen something." She glanced up and down the meadow. "Like him," she said, pointing at a shifty-looking lad of about sixteen, who was bouncing up and down on a selection of trampolines. "Sniffles Ragsdale. He's here every week, and he's always selling something different. A few weeks ago he was selling watches and clocks, and told someone he could get Big Ben for them. Then it was aquariums and rare tropical yellowfish, which nobody bought. And after that, he was selling yellowfish sushi."

The cousins and Timmy approached Sniffles' stall. There were half a dozen trampolines of different sizes, plus a selection of exercise equipment and game balls.

"And this week, it's sporting goods," Jo observed.

"Hey, Sniffles!" Dylan called as Sniffles Ragdale bounced into a somersault. "We want to talk to you!"

"Too busy," Sniffles replied, bouncing into a backward roll. "Gotta keep bouncing. Trampolines don't sell themselves."

Jo, Max, Allie and Dylan all scrambled on to other trampolines, bouncing to keep up with Sniffles.

"Have you heard of anyone trying to sell stolen plants?" Max asked. "Rare, exotic plants?"

"I'm not gonna talk," Sniffles said, bouncing down on to his bottom and up again.

Jo bounced up carrying Timmy, who growled fiercely in Sniffles' face.

"All right, I'll talk," Sniffles said, looking scared. "Word is, somebody might be looking for a buyer for a strange plant. That's all I know."

Everyone stopped bouncing except for Allie, who continued to hurtle up and down.

"So the thief is looking for a buyer!" said Max triumphantly, climbing down off his trampoline.

They suddenly heard shouting.

"Out of our way, peasants!" It was Blaine Dunston, striding through the jumble-sale crowd. He was wearing a costume crown and an armoured breastplate, a prop sword swinging at his side. "We must return home with our costumes for our party this afternoon."

His twin sister Daine minced along beside him in a conical black hat. She was carrying a large jar of glitter, which she was busy sprinkling on her face and in her hair.

"What are you coming as?" she smirked at the Five. "Oh, that's right – you're not invited."

"Crawford," Blaine called bossily over his shoulder. "Hurry up – get over here! We're ready to go home."

The mild old man in the gardening overalls scurried away from a plant stall and rushed towards his rickety old truck, his arms laden with packages.

"Hey Max, are they in your medical guide?" Jo said, nodding her head at the Dunstons as they pushed past Crawford and climbed, squabbling, into the back of his truck. "They'd make anyone sick."

"Guys?" called Allie, still bouncing up and down. "Could you help me? I can't seem to stop bouncing . . ."

As Crawford's old truck coughed and banged out of the meadow, Jo, Max and Dylan spotted a basketball hoop on a portable post that was for sale at the stall next to Sniffles'. They wheeled it next to Allie's trampoline so that she could grab on to it. Flinging out her arms mid-bounce, Allie caught hold of the hoop.

"Gee, thanks," she said in relief, doing a

gymnast's swinging dismount and landing in a heap on the grass below. "Ooof!" Allie struggled up from the grass with something sparkling all over her face and in her mouth. "I'm covered with glitter!" she spluttered, rubbing the sparkling stuff off her face.

"It must be Daine's," Jo said. "She wears so much of it she leaves a trail everywhere she goes."

Allie knelt down and studied the trail of glitter in the grass. "Hmm," she said. "Something about this looks familiar . . ."

"You're right," Max said, kneeling down beside Allie with the others. "Where have we seen this before?"

"The greenhouse!" Dylan exclaimed. "These look like the metal shavings where the lock was jimmied."

"So maybe it wasn't metal shavings," Allie gasped. "Maybe it was . . . face glitter!"

The cousins looked at each other with excitement. This was big.

"Wow!" Dylan said. "Do you think Blaine and Daine really could have stolen the bambuzu?"

"Well, I wouldn't put it past them," said Jo, getting to her feet and dusting off her hands. "They're mean enough to have done it as a trick."

"If they are the culprits," said Max, "I hope they're keeping a close eye on the bambuzu . . ."

Several miles away, the garden shed stood in a wrecked heap of wood and tangled bambuzu tendrils. The plant was snaking across the garden, wriggling through the fence and invading the next-door field of crops. On the edges of the nearby village, the bambuzu was peeking up out of

drainage grates, encircling lamp posts and post boxes.

It was out of control!

# Chapter Seven

"If it was the Dunstons," Dylan panted as he pedalled his bike hard beside the others down the twisting country road, "that explains why the thieves had a horse and cart."

"They're not old enough to drive a car, but they could drive a horse!" Allie guessed, bouncing along beside Dylan.

"Who votes we go straight to their house and see what we can find out?" called Jo over her shoulder as Timmy ran beside her, his tongue lolling pinkly from his mouth.

Wobbling slightly on their bikes, Dylan, Jo and Allie all raised their hands.

Coughing weakly as he pedalled some distance behind the others, Max said: "I think all that trampolining gave me a relapse. I think I might have Seasonal Affective Disorder, or Fin Rot, or something."

Allie squealed her bike to a halt. "Fin rot?" she demanded. "That's a fish disease! This is all in your head, Max!"

Max pedalled slowly up to Allie and stopped. "Does that mean you won't come home and take care of me again?" he said, sounding worried.

"Yes," said Allie, stamping her foot. "I've had enough!"

"Breaking news," said Dylan *sotto voce* to Jo as they straddled their bikes and waited for Allie and Max to sort themselves out. "Allie has tough side."

"I'm sorry, Max," Allie stormed, "but I'm tired of missing everything just because you think you've got something that only guppies get!"

"But what if I do have it?" Max wailed.

"I promise you I'll bury you in a shoebox or flush you down the toilet," Allie snapped. She looked at the others. "Let's go to the Dunstons. It's time to get to the bottom of this."

Jo, Allie and Dylan rode away. Timmy lolloped after them, leaving a thoughtful-looking Max following behind.

On the vast back lawn of the Dunston estate, Blaine and Daine Dunston's Wizards and Warriors party was in full swing. There were kids dressed as elves, wizards, trolls and jesters, all enjoying snacks served from medieval pavilions. Princesses bounced on an inflatable castle and knights and peasants hurtled around a little roller-coaster, while fire-breathers and jugglers prowled around and entertained the guests.

Dressed in a sort of Jedi Knight cloak, Jo emerged from some bushes alongside the iron fence surrounding the estate. She peered through the fence.

"You guys can sneak in through that drainage culvert," she said, glancing left and right. "If you can manage not to fall over, that is."

Allie and Dylan emerged from the bushes, dressed in an extraordinary dragon costume made of a green blanket sewn into a tube, with holes for their legs and a plastic dragon mask up front.

"Next time," Dylan said in a muffled voice, "I don't want to be the dragon's backside."

"It's no better being up front," Allie said, peering out of the dragon mask. "I can't see where I'm going."

The Allie-Dylan dragon took a few unsteady steps and walked into a tree trunk.

"Are you ready, Timmy?" Jo whispered.

A very small unicorn came out of the bushes and sniffed at Jo's cloak. Timmy had a costume made out

of an old sheet. There was a sharp horn fixed to his forehead, and his tail stuck out through a hole in the sheet.

"Woof!" said Timmy through the sheet.

"Good unicorn," said Jo, patting Timmy. "You guys can go through there," she said to the others, nodding at a large pipe which ran under the Dunstons' fence. "I'm climbing up that tree and getting into the house," she added, pointing at a large oak tree with limbs that stretched over the fence towards the Dunstons' large white mansion. "Anybody who finds the bambuzu, give a shout."

Timmy trotted obediently towards the pipe. The Allie-Dylan dragon followed, its front and hind ends walking out of coordination with each other.

Jo headed for the tree. Flicking her Jedi cloak over her shoulder, she scrambled up the large trunk and moved across on to a broad tree limb. The limb was massive, the twigs at its tip brushing up against a first-floor balcony on the Dunstons' house.

Snuggling down to the limb, Jo began to inch towards the balcony. The branch grew steadily

thinner. Soon, it began to bend under Jo's weight.
Then suddenly –

SNAP!

# Chapter Eight

Just ahead of Jo, the branch broke and crashed to the ground. Jo stared in horror at the stretch of air that remained between the tree and the Dunstons' balcony. It was too wide to jump.

"Too far," she groaned to herself. "Oh, I'll never get there!"

A sheepish voice spoke from the bottom of the tree.

"Will this help?"

A rubber hose with a trigger-nozzle flew up to Jo. She looked down to see Max, who had pulled the hose through the fence and tossed it up to her.

"Allie's right," Max continued as Jo caught the

hose. "It was all in my head. I'm crazy to be missing out on fun like this."

With a wide smile, Jo gave Max the thumbs-up as her cousin began to climb the tree after her. She whirled the hose around her head and flung it towards the Dunstons' balcony. The trigger-nozzle clattered on to the target and wrapped itself around the balcony struts. Jo took a deep breath. Climbing carefully hand-over-hand, she shimmied like a monkey along the hose until she reached the balcony.

Max followed. Jo held out her hand as Max came within stretching distance of the house.

TWANG!

The hose suddenly broke. Max began to fall. Jo grabbed his hand just in time and pulled him up to safety.

"Good thing you *didn't* have fin rot," she said, pulling her gasping cousin on to the balcony. "You could never have held on."

Max dusted himself off as Jo opened the balcony doors. They peered cautiously down a long upstairs hallway, lined on either side with doors leading to rooms. A staircase snaked down to the ground floor

at the balcony end of the hallway.

"Shhh," said Jo, alert. "Someone's coming!"

A nearby door opened. Jo and Max peeped through the balcony doors to see an ancient butler emerging with a tray in his hands. Very slowly, he walked away from them, down the hallway.

"We'll wait till he goes into another room," Max said.

The butler was moving extremely slowly. Jo and Max glanced at a nearby grandfather clock. It was 4.20pm.

Fifteen minutes later, the doddering butler was still too close for comfort. Max and Jo couldn't wait any longer.

"Maybe we should investigate downstairs, first," Max suggested.

Jo and Max sneaked to the staircase, taking care to move silently. The butler was still inching along, step by step. Jo put her weight on the top step. It creaked loudly. She quickly withdrew her foot and looked at her cousin. Max glanced back at the butler. They were still safe. Turning back, he noticed the banister. He waved his hands at Jo,

indicating that he planned to slide down. Jo nodded quickly.

Max sat on the banister and lifted his feet. Noiselessly, he glided down to the downstairs hall. Turning round to beam at Jo, he flew off the end and collided with a coat rack at the bottom of the stairs.

CRRAASSSHH!

Max fought off the rack as it fell on top of him, his arms and legs flailing helplessly. A pink jumper fell off one of the hooks and draped over his head.

"Aa-CHOO!" Max sneezed, wrestling with the jumper. "Aa-CHOO! AAA-CHOO!!"

"Aah," said Jo breathlessly, leaping off the end of the banister and pulling the jumper off Max's head. "Don't tell me you're allergic to wool too?"

"No," Max sniffed, his eyes watering. "I haven't sneezed like this since the greenhouse the other night."

Jo stared at Max. Then she stared at the jumper and frowned. "So . . ." she said slowly, "if you were allergic to some plant in the greenhouse, and that plant somehow got on this jumper . . ."

". . . It would make me sneeze," Max agreed. "So,

who do you suppose it belongs to?"

"It's covered with glitter," Jo said, studying the jumper. She threw a meaningful look at Max. "Who do you think?"

Outside at the Wizards and Warriors party, a juggler was tossing eight balls high in the air. Blaine and Daine Dunston were watching.

Daine, dressed up as a witchy sorceress, pulled out a hand mirror and checked her face-glitter. "You call that juggling?" she tittered. "Eight balls is nothing. Juggle this . . ." She reached over to a nearby cake stand and seized a piece of cake. Then she tossed the cake at the hapless juggler.

"And this," said Blaine, laughing as he threw an enormous cloud of candy floss at the juggler.

The juggler did his best. But the cake splattered on the ground, and soon his eight juggling balls were sticky with pink candy floss.

"Why not have him juggle some potted plants?" said Jo, approaching the Dunston twins with Max, the Allie-Dylan dragon and the Timmy-unicorn at her side.

"Yeah," said Max. "You should have plenty of them."

Blaine swung around. "What are you talking about?" he spluttered. "And what are you doing here?"

Dylan and Allie flung off their dragon costume.

"Don't act like you don't know what we're talking about," said Dylan.

Allie folded her arms. "We came to get back our aunt's bambuzu," she said.

"Your whose's what-su?" Daine said, dabbing her nose with some extra face glitter.

Jo pointed at the twins. "You broke into my mum's greenhouse," she said. "You stole her plants. We want them back."

She thrust the pink glittery jumper at Daine.

"That isn't my jumper," said Daine.

"It's got your glitter on it," Dylan accused.

Daine shrugged. "My glitter gets everywhere. It's my trademark."

"It's Mrs Crawford's jumper," said Blaine. "The groundsman's wife."

The Five stared at the Dunston twins.

"Groundsman?" said Max.

# Chapter Nine

From the midst of the wrecked garden shed in a tucked-away corner of the Dunstons' estate, the bambuzu was spreading everywhere. Thick green stalks towered over the old groundsman in tattered overalls who was trying to beat back the growth with a balding old garden broom. Beside him, his wife banged hopelessly at the plant with a leaf rake.

"Look out, dear," said Crawford. He walloped a rearing tendril of bambuzu with his broom. "There's a tendril behind you."

Mrs Crawford leaped nimbly away from the tendril, which had tried to wrap itself around her waist.

The four cousins, the Dunston twins and Timmy, who was still in his unicorn costume, came racing over the crest of a long slope toward the shed, the Crawfords and the bambuzu.

"Hey!" Jo shouted, pelting towards the old couple. "You stole my mum's bambuzu!"

Crawford's eyes widened. "The game's up, love," he said urgently to his wife. "It's time to scarper."

They dropped their garden tools and ran towards Crawford's old pick-up truck. Mrs Crawford jumped into the passenger seat as Crawford turned the ignition key. The truck spluttered into life.

"They're getting away!" Allie yelled as the truck squealed off.

Timmy raced after the clattering truck as it reversed and swung around at full speed, heading for the gate. He took a flying leap, lowering his head so his unicorn horn was pointing forward. Then he speared the rear tyre with the horn.

PFFFFT!

The tyre wobbled and sagged as the air escaped. Veering off the road, the truck drove head-first into a muddy ditch. The truck's wheels spun and there was a *bang* followed by a cloud of smoke.

"Oh, bother," said Crawford feebly from behind the steering wheel. "That didn't go so well."

The bambuzu was still growing. Thick green tendrils snaked into the ditch, drinking the muddy water greedily. More tendrils shot sky-high. Several wrapped themselves around the truck, imprisoning the Crawfords inside.

"It's getting out of control!" Max gasped, ducking as the bambuzu stems thrashed above his head. "If we don't stop it now, we never will!"

The air was filled with the crackling sound of high-speed growth. Max grabbed some lopping shears which lay in the ruins of the shed and hacked his way into the bambuzu. Allie seized a large tendril growing down through a grate. But before she could pull it out, the other end burst from a storm drain a hundred yards away and wound its way up the arm of a level-crossing gate.

TING TING TING!

Lights flashed. The gate began to lower. Allie tightened her grip and pulled, but the gate was too strong and the bambuzu began to slither from her hands.

Nearby, Dylan spritzed pesticide at another tendril which was weaving and dodging around his head like an enormous green snake. The tendril-end bunched itself into a fist and poked Dylan in the nose. His eyes watering, Dylan adopted a boxer's stance, bobbing and jabbing at the plant with his fists. It was no good. The bambuzu was the better fighter.

Elsewhere, Jo had a tendril in each hand and was trying to keep them from wrapping around her.

Meanwhile, the bambuzu was beginning to tug Allie towards the grate. Determined not to let go of her tendril, Allie dug in her heels and heaved. Something shiny winked by her feet. Looking down, Allie saw a knight's shield from the Wizards and Warriors party lying on the ground. She reached out and grabbed it, turning it towards the sun.

The sun's rays bounced off the silver shield, straight at the bambuzu, making a smouldering black hole appear in the midst of the stalks. Over at the level crossing, the bambuzu paused. Feeling the burn, it pulled back from the gate and slithered back into the storm drain. Allie fell backwards as

the tendril reversed towards the shed at high speed, slapping at the hot-spot Allie had created as it went.

Dylan was still sparring with his tendril. He was losing ground. As the tendril wound up for a final mighty punch, Allie tossed Dylan the shield. Catching it with one hand, Dylan held it over his head as the tendrils whistled towards him.

It was too late for the plant to change its small green mind.

THUMP!

The bambuzu juddered to a halt as it walloped into the shield. Shaking itself like a woozy dog, it swayed for a minute and crashed to the ground. Dylan looked pleased with himself, and dusted himself down as Timmy kicked dirt over the unconscious plant stem.

"Help!" Blaine squealed from behind Dylan.

Several new tendrils were snaking around him, wrapping him up as snugly as an insect in a spider web.

Jo tied her two tendrils together and left them to fight it out between themselves.

Then she grabbed Dylan's unconscious plant stalk and dragged it back towards the ruined shed.

Scampering up some crates on to the shed's roof, Jo tied the limp tentacle to the shed's weather vane and used it as a rope to swing down from the roof towards Blaine. She seized him under the arms and swung away from the plant, out of danger.

"Admit it," said Jo, holding Blaine as they swung out over a muddy patch of ground behind the shed. "I'm the better athlete."

"Yes, yes!" Blaine blubbered, clinging on as tightly as he could. "Fine!"

"Thanks," said Jo, and dropped Blaine into the mud.

"We can't fight it this way!" Max panted, still wielding his lopping shears as the bambuzu grew more and more stalks. "We need to get to the root of the problem!"

And he tied his handkerchief around his face and hacked his way into the centre of the shed . . .

# Chapter Ten

The main stem of the bambuzu was monstrous. It grew deep in the ground in the middle of the shed, new growth shooting out of it like jets of green rope.

Max managed to get a wrestler's hold on the vast stem. He heaved, but nothing moved.

"All right, allergy," Max roared, pulling off his handkerchief. "Do your stuff . . ."

He renewed his wrestling hold on the plant and pressed his nose to the bambuzu stem. The sneeze was coming – and it was big.

"AAH . . . AAHHH . . . **CHOOOOO!**"

The shock of the sneeze passing through Max's

body gave him the strength to tear the bambuzu stalk out at the roots. Outside, the rearing bambuzu tendrils wobbled and flopped to the ground, where at last they lay completely still. The Battle of the Bambuzu was over!

Max disentangled himself from the wreckage of the enormous plant as Jo, Dylan, Allie and Timmy poked their heads into the shed.

"Bless you!" they said.

"Woof!" added Timmy.

\* \* \*

Back in the greenhouse the following day, George carefully set a small, properly potted bambuzu plant on a table. The Five watched from a safe distance.

"There," George said, wiping her hands on her overalls. "One cutting of bambuzu, back where it belongs."

"So you're not pressing charges against Mr Crawford?" Allie asked.

"Well, he said he was sorry," George reminded Allie. "He just did it to get money so he could get out of working for the Dunstons."

"Can't blame him for that," Jo said.

George turned back to the bambuzu. She wagged her finger at the plant, whose tiny tendrils were waving gently in the warm greenhouse air. "Running amok in the countryside," she said severely. "You've been a bad boy. Or are you a girl? I don't know how to tell."

Standing just behind Allie, Max began scratching, tapping his foot and blinking rapidly. "Uh oh," he said.

Dylan rolled his eyes at the others. He turned to Max, who was scratching like mad. "Max, I hope

you're not coming down with the Bobo Virus," he said teasingly.

"It's more serious than that," Max gasped, jumping and wriggling on the spot. "I think I have MHA Syndrome."

"Here we go again," Allie sighed. "Max . . ."

Max stopped mid-wriggle and gave a smile. "MHA. 'Must Have Adventures' Syndrome," he said cheekily. "Makes me want to bike ride and climb mountains and go exploring."

Jo began scratching vigorously. "Uh-oh!" she laughed. "I have it, too!"

"So do I!" Allie giggled, blinking like crazy.

Timmy started scratching hard.

"So does Timmy," Dylan said, tapping his feet and grinning. "And so do I!"

"Well," Max said, "then there's only one cure . . ."

And with a yell, the Five burst out of the greenhouse, off in search of their next adventure.

# Epilogue

Out in the woods the following day, Max aimed Dylan's video camera at Dylan and Timmy, who were standing knee-high in the undergrowth.

"Sticky Situation Number Twelve: Poison Ivy," Max said from behind the viewfinder.

Dylan cleared his throat and looked straight at the camera. "There are a lot of plants in the woods, and some of them are poisonous," he said. "Timmy knows how to recognize poison ivy, but since he can't talk, I'll show you."

Max zoomed in on a plant.

"Poison ivy has dark glossy-green, three-part leaves, kind of palm-shaped," Dylan continued in

the background. "A good rule to remember is 'Leaves of three, let it be'."

"Woof!" Timmy jumped up and nudged Dylan on the arm.

Max swooped the camera back to Dylan. "Timmy wants me to remind people about berries," Dylan said. "Poison ivy can have clusters of white berries on it – don't eat them. Another rule: "Berries of white – take flight."

Dylan stepped back from the poison ivy plant and patted Timmy. "If you do get poison ivy on you," he informed the camera, "a favourite folk remedy is to soak yourself in a bath of oatmeal. Of course, I'm such an expert woodsman, I never touch poison ivy."

"No," said Max, still filming, "but you are standing by a clump of stinging nettles."

Dylan paled. "I am? Uh-oh . . ."

Dylan jumped away from the foliage next to him, and promptly got drenched by a heavy stream of oatmeal.

On the tree branches above, Allie and Jo were emptying the last bit of oatmeal out of two buckets.

"That'll take care of it," Allie called.

Dylan wiped a little oatmeal out of his eyes. "What's the remedy for being covered in oatmeal?" he complained.

"Timmy!" Jo laughed.

And Timmy leaped on Dylan and began to lick him all over.

### Enid Blyton

# THE
# FAMOUS FIVE'S
# SURVIVAL GUIDE

*Packed with useful information on surviving outdoors and solving mysteries, here is the one mystery that the Famous Five never managed to solve. See if you can follow the trail to discover the location of the priceless Royal Dragon of Siam.*

*The perfect book for all fans of mystery, adventure and the Famous Five!*

ISBN 9780340970836

Read the adventures of George and the
original Famous Five in